Richard Hill

Pietas Oxoniensis

A full and impartial account of the expulsion of six students from St.

Edmund Hall, Oxford. Second Edition

Richard Hill

Pietas Oxoniensis
A full and impartial account of the expulsion of six students from St. Edmund Hall,
Oxford. Second Edition

ISBN/EAN: 9783337196349

Printed in Europe, USA, Canada, Australia, Japan

Cover: Foto ©Andreas Hilbeck / pixelio.de

More available books at **www.hansebooks.com**

Pietas Oxoniensis:

OR, A

FUL AND IMPARTIAL

ACCOUNT

OF THE

EXPULSION of Six Students

from St *Edmund Hall,* OXFORD.

With a DEDICATION

To the RIGHT HONOURABLE the

Earl of *LITCHFIELD,*

CHANCELLOR of that UNIVERSITY.

By A MASTER OF ARTS
Of the UNIVERSITY of OXFORD.

Hill

Men of candor will not think that the Spirit of GOD teaches any to act direct-
ly againſt the LAWS they have *ſworn* to obſerve, and ARTICLES their
own hands have *ſubſcribed* to.

See a pamphlet intitled, A vindication of the Proceedings againſt the
Six Members of *Edmund Hall,* OXFORD.

THE SECOND EDITION,
Reviſed, Corrected and Enlarged, with ſome extraordinary Anecdotes.
To which is added, A Letter to the MONTHLY REVIEWERS.

LONDON:
Printed by J. and W. OLIVER, in *Bartholomew Cloſe*; and
Sold by G. KEITH, in *Gracechurch Street*; E. and C. DILLY, in the
Poultry; M. FOLINGSBY, at *Temple Bar*; Mr FLETCHER, at
Oxford; and to be had of any other Bookſeller in Town or Country.
MDCCLXVIII.

[Price ONE SHILLING.]

TO THE

RIGHT HONOURABLE THE

Earl of LITCHFIELD,

CHANCELLOR of the Univerſity of OXFORD,

My LORD,

YOUR Lordſhip is not only diſtinguiſhed by your illuſtrious birth and ancient family, but by a zealous attachment to the true intereſts of your King and Country. It was a deep ſenſe of your Lordſhip's worth and character, joined with the firmeſt perſuaſion of your Lordſhip's will and abilities to defend the religious and civil liberties of our Conſtitution, which cauſed our ancient Univerſity of *Oxford* ſo unanimoᵘſly to make choice of your Lordſhip to be their Chancellor; in which ſtation your Lordſhip hitherto has, and I doubt not ever will make it evidently appear, that

A 2   you

you have the profperity and welfare of the Univerfity much at heart.

Happy then may I efteem myfelf in humbly dedicating the following pages to your Lordfhip's protection and patronage; not doubting but when all the particulars relative to fome late Expulfions from that Univerfity, whereof your Lordfhip has fo eminently diftinguifhed yourfelf to be the nurfing Father, fhall be impartially fubmitted to your candor and judgment, that you will not fuffer her Laws and Privileges to be difregarded, nor any of her Members to be oppreffed or injured. And of this I am the more confident, from the polite and kind reception given by your Lordfhip to Mr Grove, (a Gentleman-Commoner of St *Edmund-Hall*, and one of the expelled Members of that Society,) when he waited upon your Lordfhip in *London*, and you teftified your approbation of his being re-admitted into the Univerfity, if the confent of Mr Vice-Chancellor and his Affeffors could be obtained: but this favour being denied, Mr Grove did not choofe to give your Lordfhip any further trouble.

However

However the late sentence may have the appearance of an Univerfity-Act, or however it may pafs for fuch in hiftory, when children's children fhall read the dire account, yet it is the higheft injuftice to that ancient and refpectable feminary of true piety and learning to look upon it in this light; for befides that only four Heads of Houfes were prefent upon the occafion, I am well affured that many great and eminent men in the Univerfity have teftified their difapprobation that matters were carried with fo high an hand: particularly the Reverend and Learned Doctor DIXON, Principal of the Hall from whence thefe fix Students were expelled, (who, it muft be allowed, was the beft judge of their characters and conduct) fpoke of them in the higheft terms before the whole Court; and has fince told me himfelf, that he never remembers in his own, or in any other College, fix youths whofe lives were fo exemplary, and who behaved themfelves in a more humble, regular, peaceable manner.

How far thefe fix members have or have not deferved the fhameful and fevere punifh-

ment

ment inflicted upon them, the following
sheets will enable your Lordship and the
world to judge. I shall only add, that I
have been particularly careful not to assert
any thing upon hearsay evidence, but have
taken much pains to trace up every circum-
stance and fact that I have alledged, to the
fountain-head, which has caused the publication of the piece to be deferred longer
than was intended.

I am,

My LORD,

Your Lordship's most obedient humble Servant,

June 1, 1768.

A MASTER OF ARTS
of the University of OXFORD.

PIETAS OXONIENSIS:

OR, A

FULL AND IMPARTIAL

ACCOUNT, &c.

ONSCIOUS of the mighty power of prejudice, and how apt men are to be influenced by an undue regard to Names, Sects, and Parties, before I enter upon the following work, I think it neceffary to acquaint the reader, that I am a member of the Eftablifhed Church, into whofe communion I was in my infancy baptized, and for whofe doctrine and difcipline I ftill pro-

fefs

fefs the higheft veneration. It is not therefore in behalf of this or that denomination of chriftians that I attempt to write; the caufe of religion in general, and that of the Church of *England* in particular, the caufe of violated truth, trampled laws, and injured innocence, is what I mean to defend. And as I would not be biafed by an attachment to any parties, 'fo neither to any perfons. As to the fix young men who have been lately expelled from *Edmund Hall*, I had very little acquaintance with any of them, and fome of them were totally unknown to me, till after their Sentence was paffed, fo that I am in lefs danger of partiality on that account; and can appeal to the fearcher of hearts, that I defire to be guided by a fpirit of wifdom, truth, love and candor, in what I have undertaken; as alfo to have every word I advance to be weighed in the balance of calm reflection and of unbiafed judgment; and if plain undifguifed truth fhould be found to bear hard, perhaps very hard, upon fome individuals, this is neither the fault of the truth itfelf, nor of thofe who bring it to light.

THE firft trace which I can difcover of any diffatisfaction againft thefe fix Gentlemen, was an application of the Rev. Mr H—N, their Tutor, to the Rev. Doctor D—N, Principal of the Hall. The charge was, " That there were feveral Enthufiafts in that fociety, who talked of regene-
" ration,

" ration, infpiration, and drawing nigh unto God."
Doctor D. well knowing that the Gentleman who
brought the accufation, had long laboured under
an infanity of mind, for which he had been obliged
to leave the Univerfity, and undergo the difcipline
in fuch cafes neceffary ; and confidering that he was
withal of a very proud revengeful difpofition, juftly
imagined that what he faid might be partly the
effect of his diforder, or partly owing to fome
pique he had taken againft the young men ; he
therefore thought that the lefs he argued the cafe
with him (at that period) the better, and only obferved, that thefe were all fcriptural phrafes or
apoftolical expreffions, and the ufe of them au-
thorifed by the offices of the Church of *England*,
that therefore he could fee no caufe to look upon
the Gentlemen as enthufiafts for having adopted
thefe terms *.

Let none fuppofe from what I have faid that I
mean to reflect upon Mr H. on account of the vi-
fitation he has been under in the deprivation of
his

* *John* iii. 3, 5, 6, &c. " Jefus anfwered, Except a man
" be born again he cannot fee the kingdom of God," &c.—
Collect for Chriftmas day. " Grant that we being regenerate,
" and made thy children by adoption and grace, may daily be
" renewed by thy holy Spirit," &c.—Communion Service.
" Cleanfe the thoughts of our hearts by the inspiration of thy
" holy Spirit," &c.—Collect for the fifth Sunday after Eafter.
" Grant, that by thy holy Inspiration we may think thofe
" things that be good." The Apoftle James exhorts us to
draw nigh unto God ; and his Brother Paul bids us, *draw near
in full affurance of faith.*

his fenfes, GOD forbid! fo far from it, that whilft I really feel the fincereft pity for him, I look upon this as the beft excufe which can be offered for his conduct ; and if others have taken advantage of this poor unhappy Gentleman, in order to make him the tool or cat's-paw to perpetrate what, through fhame or fear, they durft not undertake themfelves, however this may exempt him from reflections, as an object truly meriting compaffion, yet it will not exempt any who were the firft movers in this bufinefs, and much lefs thofe who have fuffered themfelves to be fo far led and in-fluenced by him, as to pafs the moft cruel, igno-minious fentence which can poffibly be inflicted by the Univerfity-laws, in great meafure upon his fingle evidence, or elfe by letters he had received from others ; which letters, it will plainly appear, were ftuffed with the groffeft falfhoods and mif-reprefentations ; yet were thefe letters*, and this evidence,

*. Among the letters read at the *trial,* as it is called, of thefe Students, was one which had been intercepted from a religious youth to his friend, wherein the title of King was applied to the name of JESUS, which expreffion the Rev. Mr H. read in a manner which befpoke the higheft contempt; and which raifed a loud unbecoming laughter among the gownfmen prefent. Truly fhocking muft it found to a chriftian ear, to hear the kingly office of the Saviour of finners thus turned into ridicule, and this, by whom, before whom, and in what place, *borrendum dictu!* But the language of every natural heart is, " We will not have this man to reign over us ; we have no " King but Cefar."—An expreffion from the Rev. Mr HAWEIS was alfo brought on the carpet, concerning which the faid

Clergyman

evidence, admitted as much as if they had amount-
ed to full incontestible proofs, and in the most
unprecedented, illegal, arbitrary manner, all the
witnesses against the parties accused were examined
without being put to their oath (except one, namely,
the Rev. Mr GREAVES, a worthy conscientious
man, who was justly supposed to be their friend:)
and not only was, whatever these witnesses advanced from their own personal knowledge, but
likewise every idle report they had picked up by
hear-say, admitted as genuine, and charged upon
these young men; who were even compelled to turn
their own accusers, or else condemned for contu-
macious behaviour, in a manner which exceeded
the dreadful tyrannical oath EX OFFICIO, which
was administered to the Nonconformists by the
High-Commission Court in Queen ELIZABETH's
time, or the proceedings of the Star-Chamber and
the same High-Commission-Court in the two following reigns † : insomuch that I will venture to
appeal

Clergyman actually asked, (by way of exposing the term)
whether Mr HAWEIS did not say, that "Mr MIDDLETON was
"a dear child of GOD?" What a dreadful pass indeed are
things come to, when the endearing comfortable relation in
which GOD stands to the believing sinner, as his reconciled
Father in CHRIST, and a phrase which is used at least an
hundred times in scripture (namely, that of a child of GOD) as
well as in various parts of the offices of our own Church, is
made matter of scoff and reproach?

† These Courts were abolished by Act of Parliament in the
reign of CHARLES I, as favoring so very strongly of Popish
Inquisition.

appeal to every man who is at all acquainted with
the fpirit of our laws, and the liberty of our con-
ftitution, whether both Law and Juftice, not to
fay *Religion* and *Confcience*, were not as much put
out of the queftion in this tranfaction, as if they
had never had any exiftence.

But to proceed.——Mr H. being much diffatisfied
with Dr D's anfwer in vindication of the young
men, began to fet other engines to work for their
overthrow; he wrote to different Clergymen, who
lived in the fame parifhes, or in the neighbourhood
of thefe young men, and from them received
particular accounts of all their proceedings, em-
bellifhed and interlarded according to the fancies
and ingenuity of the refpective writers. One of
thefe Clergymen, who was then Curate of *New-
port* in *Shropfhire*, and lately fhewed himfelf a
zealous champion for a company of ftrolling Play-
ers, in oppofition to a neighbouring Juftice of the
Peace who fent thofe pefts of fociety out of the
town*, took the pains of going to a village called
Wheaton-

---

* This juftice of the peace told the fame Clergyman in a
private letter he wrote to him upon the fubject, that " any
" chriftian Divine might blufh at the thought of encouraging
" a gang of idle ftrollers by his prefence and purfe, in direct
" oppofition to magiftracy." In anfwer to which letter the
Clergyman replied, (as I faw it under his own hand) that
" though he faw no caufe to blufh for himfelf, he faw caufe to
" blufh for the Magiftrate who cenfured him for countenancing
" and

Wheaton-Afton in *Staffordfhire*, to gather what intelligence he could concerning Mr JONES, one of the fix expelled Students, who ufed to vifit a pious Gentlewoman of the Church of *England* at that place, and now and then, at her requeft, performed the family-worfhip, to which the poor neighbours were admitted; when Mr JONES read and explained part of a chapter in the Bible, and afterwards prayed and fung a Pfalm or Hymn with them. The way whereby Mr BLACKHAM, the Clergyman abovementioned, came to the knowledge of this, was, by calling on fome ferious perfons who were prefent on thefe occafions, and pretending a fingular regard and affe6tion for Mr JONES, and the higheft approbation of his conduct; the artlefs people foon furnifhed him with fufficient matter for an anfwer to his letter, which anfwer was accordingly produced in court, with the addition of a letter which Mr JONES had fome years ago written to this Clergyman, upon his having fent him Dr TRAPP's Sermons upon *the danger of being righteous over-much*, a danger which this Divine, to do him juftice, is as careful to avoid,

" and attending the ftrollers, from whofe performances he " drew real advantage."

The holy and learned Dr EDWARDS, in his excel'ent book intitled the Preacher, page 100, taking it for granted that no Clergyman would be feen in a play-houfe, yet tells the Clergy that if their Auditors be addi6ted to plays, they will not care for their fermons, unlefs the fermons be akin to the plays.

avoid, as the unpardonable fin againſt the holy Ghoſt.

BUT as the particular charges againſt each of theſe Gentlemen will be beſt ſeen by the ſeveral Articles for which they were expelled, I proceed to conſider theſe Articles one by one, as nearly as they can poſſibly be recollected ; and if in any thing they ſhould vary from the Originals, which however I believe they do not in the leaſt point, the fault is not mine, but theirs who refuſed a copy of theſe Articles to the young men them-ſelves, after they had expelled them. But where-fore was this requeſt denied ? if the ſentence was juſt, why ſhould the reaſons for which it was in-flicted be huddled up and kept ſecret, eſpecially from thoſe who were the unhappy ſufferers by it ? if they had done amiſs, could there be a better method of convincing them of it, and of preſerv-ing them from the like faults for the time to come, than by giving each of them a copy of the charges on which they were proceeded againſt ? If it be ſaid, that the Articles of their accuſation were included in the ſummons fixed upon the Chapel-door; I anſwer, that the charges contained in the ſummons were in a more vague general ſtile than thoſe on which they were ſeparately arraigned and expelled; beſides, it is not what a perſon is accuſed of, or ſummoned to anſwer to, but what he is lawfully convicted of, that will render him liable

to

to punifhment in any nation where Tyranny and Defpotifm are not the avowed principles of government *.

The Articles, as nearly as can be recollected, ftand as follows.

I. JAMES MATTHEWS was bred a Weaver, and kept a common Tap-houfe. When he entered himfelf a member of the Univerfity, he had not fuch a competent knowledge in the learned languages as would enable him to perform the exercifes of the Hall and of the Univerfity. — He hath applied for Orders, and hath been refufed.—He ftill remains incapable

---

* Mr GROVE and Mr MIDDLETON went to the V—C—— after their expulfion, and defired a copy of the Articles for which they were expelled ; but this favour was refufed : however Mr V—C——intimated that " he thought it was right to give them a copy, but that the other heads of houfes were againft it ; and that for his part he was concerned that he was in office to pafs fuch a fentence upon them; and if the matter had depended upon him, he fhould have been for lefs violent methods." Now Mr V—C—— might perhaps think that by this foothing fpeech to the young men in private, he fhould fhake off a little dirt from himfelf; but how agrees this difcourfe with his publicly thanking Mr H—N for the fervice he had done the U——y ? Befides, if Mr V—C—— really thought the fentence fo very hard and fevere, why did he pafs it? Ought he, for the fake of obliging any perfons whatever, to inflict a punifhment upon fix pious harmlefs youths, which, for ought he knew, might reduce them to the very want of bread, and caft a lafting ftigma upon their names and characters ?

capable of performing the exercises of the said Hall, much less of taking holy Orders. —He hath frequented unlawful Conventicles, by his own confession.—He hath been with Mr DAVIES and one Mr FLETCHER, reputed Methodists, and is himself a reputed Methodist.

II. THOMAS JONES was bred a Barber, and hath lately followed that low occupation. —— He hath expounded the Scriptures at *Wheaton-Aston*, although a Layman. He hath attended illicit Conventicles in this city, as appears from his own confession.—He is deficient in the learned languages.

III. JOSEPH SHIPMAN was bred a Linen-draper, is deficient in learning, and hath attended illicit Conventicles.

IV. BENJAMIN KAY hath attended illicit Conventicles at a private house it this city.—Hath heard one HEWET, a Stay-maker, although a Layman, pray extempore.—He holds Election: if once a child of GOD, always a child of GOD: and that the influence of the Spirit is necessary to constitute every one a child of GOD.—He has endeavoured to draw others into these opinions.

V. ERASMUS

V. Erasmus Middleton has officiated as Prieſt in a Chapel of eaſe belonging to the Pariſh-church of *Chevely*, in the county of *Berks* and dioceſe of *Saliſbury*, as appears by his own confeſſion.—He ſays, we muſt ſit down and wait for the Spirit, for without it we can do nothing.—That good Works are unneceſſary, and no part of our juſtification, but that we are ſaved by Faith alone.

VI. Thomas Grove hath, by his own confeſſion, preached to a mixed multitude of people called Methodiſts in a barn, and offered up extempore Prayer.

For which crimes we, David Durell, D. D. Vicechancellor of the Univerſity and Viſitor of the Hall ; Thomas Randolph, D. D. Preſident of *C. C. C* ; Thomas Fothergil, D. D. Provoſt of *Queens-College* ; Thomas Nowel, D. D. Principal of St *Mary-Hall*, and the Reverend Thomas Atterbury, A. M. of *Chriſt-Church*, Senior Proctor, deem each of them worthy of being expelled the Hall ; I therefore by my viſitatorial power do hereby pronounce them expelled *.

Beſides all theſe charges there was added that of impudence and diſobedience towards their Tutor, and leaving College without his leave.

B   IN

* This ſentence was pronounced in the Chapel.

IN order to proceed with the greater method and perspicuity, we will first consider the charge of attending illicit Conventicles, of which they were most of them found guilty ; particularly Mr GROVE, of preaching in a barn.

2dly, The charge against JAMES MATTHEWS, JOSEPH SHIPMAN and THOMAS JONES, concerning their having been bred to Trades.

3dly, The charge against JAMES MATTHEWS, JOSEPH SHIPMAN and THOMAS JONES, for being insufficient in the learned languages.

4thly, The charge against ERASMUS MIDDLETON, for having officiated in a chapel unordained.

5thly, The charge against BENJAMIN KAY and ERASMUS MIDDLETON, for holding the doctrines of Election, Perseverance, Justification by Faith alone without Works, and that we can do nothing without the Spirit of GOD ; into which opinions the said BENJAMIN KAY is also found guilty of having endeavoured to draw others.

6thly, The charge against JAMES MATTHEWS and others, for being acquainted with reputed Methodists, Mr VENN, Mr NEWTON, Mr TOWNSEND, and particularly with Mr FLETCHER and Mr DAVIES.

Firſt

First then, with regard to the charge of attending illicit Conventicles.—Now in order to prove who are and who are not guilty of this offence, it is necessary first to ascertain what is a Conventicle.—Mr J ACOB, in his *Law-Dictionary*, observes, "That the word was first attributed to the Meetings of W ICKLIFF in this nation, and is now applicable to *the illegal Meetings of the Nonconformists*." And the preamble to the Act of 22 C AR. II. cap. 1. gives a very full and clear insight into the Act itself, and against what persons it was designed. It begins as follows —" For providing further and more speedy remedies against the growing and dangerous practices of seditious Sectaries, and other disloyal persons, who, under pretence of tender consciences, have or may at their meetings contrive insurrections (as late experience has shewn) be it enacted," &c. &c. &c.

The design of the LXXIIId Canon of our Church is entirely to prevent any secret meetings, particularly among the Clergy, "to consult upon any matter which may tend to the impeaching and depraving the doctrine of the Church of *England*, or the book of Common Prayer, or of any part of the government and discipline now established in the Church of *England*."

The

The Statute of the University, *De Conventiculis
illicitis* * *reprimendis*, is in every respect conform-
able to the Canon and Act of Parliament. " Sta-
" tutum eft quod nullus cujuſcunque gradus, five
" ſtatus, conventicula illicita intra Univerſitatis
" præcinctum inſtituat aut iis quo modo interſit,
" aut in domo vel hoſpitio ſuo haberi permittat.
" Qualia cenſenda ſunt in quibus contra pacem
" publicam, doctrinam vel diſciplinam eccleſiæ
" vel regimen et tranquilitatem Univerſitatis quic-
" quam deliberatum vel geſtum fuerit : vel in
" quibus homines (ſecus quam ſtatutis Regni, ca-
" nonibus eccleſiæ, vel ordinationibus Univerſi-
" tatis permittitur) vel palam vel occulte con-
" veniunt."

Now from all theſe authorities it is moſt clear
that there is no prohibition laid on any Members
of the Church of *England* for meeting together
for religious purpoſes, provided ſuch meeting
tend not " to the impeaching and depraving the
" doctrine of the Church of *England*, the book of
" Common Prayer, the public peace, nor any part
" of

---

* The word ILLICIT is evidently uſed to ſhew us, that there
is a difference and diſtinction to be made between Conventicles
which are lawful and unlawful. The word Conventicle (from
Convenio) plainly means a gathering together, and where this
is only of members of the Eſtabliſhed Church, though it ſhould
be in a private houſe or elſewhere, neither the Act of parliament,
the 73d Canon, nor the Univerſity-Statute, give any authority
to call it an *illicit* Conventicle.

" of the government and difcipline eftablifhed in
" the Church."—The Act of Parliament, it is evident, was made to prevent difloyal, feditious,
fchifmatical affemblies, among fuch as, *under pretence of tender confciences*, refufed to conform to
the eftablifhed communion : but not a fingle example can be found of this Act ever having been
put in execution againft members of the Church
of *England*, nor was it ever fuppofed to have the
leaft reference to fuch, till fome malicious perfons
of late attempted to proceed againft a few pious
people, if I miftake not, in the County of *Kent*,
who were affembled together in a private houfe
for their fpiritual edification ; but an appeal to the
Court of *Kings-bench* being determined on, the
juftice of peace who granted the warrant and
levied the penalty, acknowledged his error, and
made fatisfaction to the plaintiffs ; fo the matter
was made up, as I am informed from one of the
Attornies employed in the caufe ; and indeed
the very reafon and nature of the thing prove
the illegality of the Magiftrate's proceeding, as
it would be the higheft reflection upon the wifdom of the Legiflature, to imagine a Law had
paffed, whereby perfons of the eftablifhed communion would be under greater reftrictions than
the Diffenters themfelves. A Law which would
prohibit all members of the Church, from joining
together in prayer for the welfare of that Church,
unlefs it were within the confecrated walls. And

if

if upon any occafion there happened to be half a
dozen guefts or ftrangers prefent at the ftated family worfhip in a houfe, if but a prayer was
offered up (unlefs it were one taken out of the
Liturgy) a Pfalm fung, or a Chapter read, whoever pleafed (even a menial fervant) might turn
informer, and the whole company would be liable
to the penalties of an illicit conventicle.

A further proof that this Act was not intended to prevent members of the Church of
England from meeting together for the advancement of piety, may be gathered from the Religious Societies eftablifhed in Queen ANNE's time,
as we have the account of them publifhed by the
Rev. Dr Jos. WOODWARD; the members of which
Societies ufed frequently to affemble together, to
the amount of a large number, for Prayer, Reading, finging Hymns, &c. " And in this happy
" and bleffed work, faith the Doctor in his Pre-
" face, we have in many places in this nation,
" efpecially in our capital city, perfons of no mean
" rank and quality effectually engaged, through
" the great mercy of GOD to us; namely, Lords
" Spiritual and Temporal, Baronets, Knights,
" Efquires, Members of the Honourable Houfe
" of Commons, Juftices of the Peace, Minifters
" and Gentlemen, together with Aldermen and
" Citizens of all ranks, Officers of divers ftations,
" and private perfons of all forts." For this the
Doctor

Doctor is thankful, and esteems it a signal mercy
of God to our land; but what encouragement
these zealous Christians would have met with in
our day, sad experience too plainly shews.

If it be said, that though these six young men
may not have offended against the letter of the
Act of Parliament, the LXXIIId Canon of the
Church, nor the Statute of the University, yet as
they knew that what they did was displeasing to
their Seniors and Governors, they ought to have
abstained from it. I answer, That they did ab-
stain as soon as ever they were told that their meetings were contrary to the will of those who had
the authority over them in the University; and
not one of them had been present at any such
meetings for some months before their expulsion,
but all declared it was their determination not to
attend them again; nay, they had even their
Tutor's advice in every step they took, as well in
their meetings at first, as in their absenting themselves from them afterwards; particularly was this
the case with Mr Jones in his meeting a few religious people at *Wheaton Aston* in *Staffordshire* †;

B 4 not-

---

† About three or four months before Mr Jones was sum-
moned to appear in Court, his Tutor told him that he had
heard of his preaching or expounding in fields, barns, &c. and
desired to know if it was true. Mr Jones replied that he would
tell him the whole that he had done, and then he might call it
preaching or whatever he pleased.—" That when he was at a
" relation's

notwithstanding which this most cruel and igno·
minious sentence was pronounced against them ;
concerning which I shall only observe, that though
it is now near twenty Years since I commenced a
member

" relation's house in *Staffordshire*, where there was constant fa-
" mily worship, (to which the neighbours of the Village were
" admitted) he sometimes read out of Bishop Beveridge's
" private Thoughts, and sometimes read and explained part
" of a chapter in the Bible, after which there was Prayer and
" an Hymn. But that as to what had been said concerning
" his preaching in barns or fields, it was utterly false, such ir-
" regularities being contrary to his judgment, as he hoped to be
" regularly ordained a Minister of the established Church."

Mr Jones then asked his Tutor if there was any harm in
this; to which he replied, " God knows, I don't know that
" there is any harm in it; it is very well for people to instruct
" their neighbours, provided there is no Enthusiasm in it."
Mr Jones added, " Sir if you think what I do is wrong, I de-
" sire you will tell me plainly, as I expect to go into *Stafford-
" shire* at the Vacation, and may probably do the same again."
—To this Mr Higson made the same answer as before, and
told Mr Jones, he was glad that what he had heard concerning
him was false ; and so they parted.

Notwithstanding this conversation between Mr Jones and
his Tutor, yet the latter told the Court that he had forbid Mr
Jones going to meetings, without effect.—Mr Jones then begged
to be heard in his own behalf, and related all the above dis-
course, which the Tutor knowing in his conscience to be true,
could make no reply to. — Upon this Mr Jones told Mr
V— C—— " That he hoped he would remember that he was
" accused of nothing but what he had declared to his Tutor
" three or four months before :" to which Dr Nowel an-
swered, with a sneering laugh, " Yes, yes, we will remember it."
—And truly it was *remembered* to be made an heavy article
against Mr Jones, and part of the charge read at his Expulsion.

member of the University, and during the time
of my residence it has been frequently discovered
that young men have lain out at nights, and that
both young and old had lewd women come to them
in college, who have fathered children * on them,
and that others have been guilty of Drunkennefs,
Rioting, Gaming, insolent Behaviour to Proctors
in the execution of their magisterial office, &c.
&c. &c. yet I never remember one instance of
expulsion for all or any of these crimes, and believe the only example which can be produced
within these hundred years † of so public an in-
fliction of a like punishment was upon Mr——,
for the horrible blasphemous crime of administer-
ing the holy Sacrament to an Ass, to which were
added several other enormities too dreadful to
mention. Upon a level with these crimes, *hor-
refco*

---

* If required, I can produce two instances of this in reverend
Fellows of Colleges, who had each an illegitimate child laid to
their account by two dirty Apple-women, who used to attend
the Colleges. But these events only occasioned a little common-
room mirth.

† However rare expulsions for Sin may be, we have several
instances of expulsions for the faith and practice of primitive
Christianity. About the year 1367, JOHN WICKLIFF, the
morning star of the Reformation, was ejected from the War-
denship of *Canterbury Hall* in *Oxford*, (now swallowed up in
Christ-Church College) and three of his followers were turned
out of their Fellowships, for the cause of the Gospel. And
about the year 1382, WILLIAM COURTNEY, then Archbishop of
Canterbury, sent a letter to the Vicechancellor, Proctors, and
heads of Houses, requiring them to expel all favorers of
WICKLIFF's doctrine from the University.

refce referens l. is ranked that of Reading, Praying Extempore, and expounding the Scriptures
in a private houfe *.

    Mr Grove was not charged upon the trial with
preaching in a barn, and did not hear any thing of
it till the V—C——, and his affeffors came to the
Chapel to read the fentence of Expulfion. Upon
Mr Grove's hearing this accufation, he affirmed
that it was falfe. Mr V—C—— being afked
what Mr Grove faid, anfwered, that he denied
the fact ; however he was put down guilty of it,
by Dr N—l, and fentence was accordingly pafs-
ed upon him, though he really never did it, and
abfolutely denied it.

    COME we now to the fecond charge againft
thefe young men ; namely, that three of them
were bred to trades. One of them, Mr James
Matthews, it is acknowledged, was bred a Clo-
thier, but not a *Weaver*, and afterwards lived with
his elder Brother, who kept a reputable inn.
Here he remained no long while, but retired to the
houfe of a learned Clergyman, under whofe in-
ftructions he ftudied and prepared himfelf for the
miniftry before he entred at the Univerfity.—
Mr Thomas Jones, it is granted, was once (tho'

not

* A Gentleman who was a member of the College where this
horrible crime was committed, has fince told me, that it was
done in the very Chapel, or Antichapel, but that the Blafphemer
came off with a punifhment far fhort of Expulfion ; namely, that
of being denied a Fellowfhip.

not *lately*) a Perukemaker, and that Mr Joseph Shipman, was for a short time with a Linen-draper‡. And are these crimes which deserve the most severe punishment that an U———— y can inflict ? If our blessed Lord deigned himself to be a Carpenter, and the son of a Carpenter, and to take poor illiterate Fishermen to be workers together with him in the ministry of the Gospel; if the great Apostle of the *Gentiles* laboured with his own hands at the business of Tent-making; if David, the man after God's own heart, was called from the sheepfold to be a prophet in *Israel*; if Amos himself confesseth that he was no prophet, neither a prophet's son, but an herdman and gatherer of sycamore fruit, and that the Lord took him as he followed the flock, and said unto him, " Go, prophecy unto my people *Israel**;" surely there is nothing so very culpable or absurd in any person becoming a candidate for holy orders, who in the former part of his life followed an honest profession.

It was observed in some of our news-papers, in answer to this charge, that the great Cardinal Wolsey was brought up in a Butcher's shop, and that

---

‡ Had Mr Shipman pursued this business, he had a prospect of gaining a considerable fortune ; but being religiously disposed, he chose to sacrifice worldly ease and profit, that he might labour in his Master's vineyard, and would have thought himself happy, and highly honoured in the possession of a small Curacy.　　　　* Amos vii. 15.

that a late eminent Prelate was bred a Paſtry-cook;
to which may be added, that another very great
Dignitary in the Church, whoſe piety, modera-
tion, and candor in that ſtation have few equals,
was educated in the profeſſion of Phyſic, and had
taken the degree of M. D. before he changed the
courſe of his ſtudies *. That great German Divine and Reformer, WOLFANGUS MUSCULUS, was
ſon of a poor Cooper, and obliged to ſing from
door to door for ſubſiſtence ; and I am well
aſſured, that one of the late Rev. Proctors of the
Univerſity was for ſome time a Lieutenant in the
Army ; and that the gentleman himſelf who
brought this accuſation againſt the young men,
either now has, or once had a Curate near *Bath*,
who was a Packer, Carrier, Waggoner, or ſome
ſuch low occupation ; and has been heard to boaſt
how many Churches the ſaid dextrous Curate
could ſerve in one day.

THE third charge comes now to be conſidered,
namely, that three of theſe young men, *viz.* Mr
MATTHEWS, Mr JONES, and Mr SHIPMAN, were
deficient in the knowledge of the learned languages.—One would think that the abſurdity of
this accuſation muſt ſtrike every one at firſt ſight ;
for if they were any of them backward in their
ſtudies, was not this the beſt reaſon in the world
why

* See the account of the late Archbiſhop of C—— as
given in the public papers, particularly that in St JAMES's
Chronicle. N° 1163, from Auguſt 11, to Auguſt 13.

why they fhould be fuffered to purfue them? And can their Tutor deny that they had made confiderable progrefs in their learning fince they entred at the Hall? And if then before they were known to be religious, they were deemed fufficiently qualified to be admitted members of the Univerfity, why were they afterwards expelled under pretence of infufficiency in the learned languages, when they not only had made but were making great advancement in the knowledge of thofe languages? To adopt the fentiment of a paragraph I faw in the papers, " What fhould we think of thofe " who were for removing food from a man be- " caufe he was hungry, or fire becaufe he was " cold? Yet juft the fame part do they act, who " drive a man from the feat of learning and im- " provement, becaufe he is yet deficient in the " knowledge of the languages." But neither can this deficiency be attributed to them all. Mr MIDDLETON paffed his examination honourably, and offered to produce copies of all his College exercifes. Another of them, Mr KAY, muft be acknowledged by his moft bitter enemies to be well fkilled in academical learning. A third begged to be excufed paffing an examination at that time, on account of the agitation his mind was in before the Court, yet he was put down infufficient: But let me appeal to every candid perfon, whether this was a fit time to make trial of their literary abilities, when any man who had not an extraordinary

nary

nary degree of effrontery must needs find himself under much confusion and discompofure ?— Doctor D—n, their Principal, obferved to Mr V—C---r, that if others were queftioned concerning their knowledge in the learned languages, it would appear that very many were equally, if not more deficient than any of the fix expelled Gentlemen: But none of thofe, whom Dr D—n was defirous of having examined, were accufed of the crime of being *righteous over-much*, and therefore they were not called upon. However, if the Tutor himfelf will pleafe to recollect, he will find that he now has, and at the very fame period had, a certain illiterate pupil *, who has a wife and children,

---

* Befides this Gentleman, Mr H. had introduced two or three other pupils of the fame ftamp, particularly one Mr —— , who, though he has been at a public fchool, and is now more than four years ftanding in the U——y, is equally deficient in the learned languages with any of the young men who were expelled ; and feldom, if ever, attends the Tutor's lectures ; but as this Gentleman is contented with a very moderate fhare of Religion, there was no accufation againft him.

Mr B——t was another of Mr H——'s Pupils, whom he himfelf brought to the Hall before Dr Dixon was Principal ; and often boafted that he taught him the firft rudiments of Grammar at the U——y ; but this Gentleman being neither addicted to finging of hymns, admonifhing his neighbours, or ufing extempore prayer, was never objected againft.

Let me afk the Rev. Mr A——, one of the affeffors who fat in judgment upon the young men, whether he himfelf did not fome time ago admit an exhibitioner from *Bridgenorth* in *Shropfhire* to *Chrift Church*, whom he knew to be exceedingly illiterate,

dren, the eldeſt of whom is lately come to age,
which pupil he deſired might be admitted a member of the Hall, when between thirty and forty
years old, that he might juſt keep his terms, and
get into Orders; yet there is no accuſation at all
againſt him, his age, ignorance, and former occupation, are not in the leaſt excepted againſt;
nor is he at all ſuppoſed to be ſent to the Univerſity for the ſake of SKULKING INTO ORDERS *;
nay, ſo far was this Gentleman from being under
any odium or reproach for theſe things, that at his
houſe the Tutor furniſhed himſelf with his evidence againſt Mr GROVE.

Among the witneſſes examined againſt the
young men, was a candidate for holy Orders of
the ſame Society, who, it appeared upon the trial,
had aſſerted, "that whoſoever believed the mira-
"cles of our SAVIOUR or of MOSES, muſt be a
"knave or a fool," or words to the like import,
and is well known in the Hall by the name of
THE INFIDEL §.—However his teſtimony againſt
the

rate, more ſo than any of the ſix expelled Students; and who
being aſked how many conjugations there were in the Greek
language, could not reſolve the queſtion.

* This expreſſion was uſed in the news papers concerning
the ſix young men.

§ Some of this Gentleman's friends were afterwards ſo kind
as to make an apology for him to Mr V—C—— by ſaying,
that he had got diſguiſed in liquor at St JOHN's Gaudy, when
he made that unfortunate ſpeech. Now this Gaudy (or
guttling

the fix ftudents was received as if it had been as
true as that Gofpel which he defpifes, nor does he
meet with any moleftation in the enjoyment of
his principles; but I doubt not will find plenty
of Reverend friends to fign his Teftimonials, and
to witnefs to the *orthodoxy* of his doctrine and the
piety of his life: though it is hoped that Mr V—
C——, if it is but for the fake of faving appear-
ances, will at leaft give him fome rebuke, and
make that rebuke as public as the fentence pronounced againft the other fix members‡.

I now

guttling day) is held in memory of the abftemious St John
Baptift; but as Mr W—n does not honor that Saint by believ-
ing his teftimony, he pays him the compliment of getting drunk.
—*In vino veritas.*

Permit me here to inquire whether a certain fleek Divine,
who not long fince excited the rifible faculties of his learned au-
dience by preaching up Mortification, and who has fhewn himfelf
a warm advocate for the doctrine of Juftification by works, and
as warm an enemy to the expelled members, did not alfo get
very ROCKY in honour of the Church, on *Friday* the eleventh
day of *March* 1768, being the memorable night on which the
fix young fanatics were caft out of the Univerfity.

‡ Although I would not affert that Mr V—C——, or any
of the heads of houfes, prefer Infidelity to what is called Methodifm, yet fince the firft edition of this pamphlet went to the
prefs, Mr W. who made the horrible affertion concerning the
miracles of our Lord and of Mofes, has been convened before
them, and after going through the farce of afking pardon in
Latin for what he had faid, was difmiffed with a reprimand. And
although none of the religious Youths who were expelled, have
been fuffered to enter again at any other College, notwithftanding the Chancellor fo gracioufly and candidly gave them permiffion

I now proceed to the charge againſt Mr MID-
DLETON, for having officiated in' a Chapel unordained: And here, though I muſt believe his
motive to have been good, for he could have no
temporal intereſt in what he did, yet I condemn
the action as a very high indiſcretion, and a fla-
grant violation of the Twenty-third Article of our
church; and indeed he himſelf has long acknowledged it to be ſo †, and proved the ſincerity of
this acknowledgement by behaving ever ſince with
the greateſt regularity. But though I would impartially cenſure the great imprudence of this ſtep
in Mr M. yet how can his moſt prejudiced enemies
defend the proceeding againſt him, even to Expulſion itſelf, for an offence which was committed

C

a long

miſſion to do ſo, if the conſent of the V— C——, &c. could
be obtained, yet in order to caſt a greater ſtigma and oppro-
brium upon *Edmund* Hall, and the worthy Principal of it,
ſeveral members of that Society have been ſuffered to take
their names out of the Books, and to enter at *Magdalen* Hall;
and this after Mr V— C—— had told Mr GROVE, and
ſolemnly given his word to the Principal, that unleſs the expelled young men were received again into the U ——y,
none of the others ſhould have liberty to leave his Hall and to
enter elſewhere.—*Heu! priſca! fides!*

By the expulſion of the ſix young men, and this permiſſion
being given to the others to leave the Hall, Doctor DIXON,
the Principal, is deprived of great part of his uſual income:
and this treatment he hath met with notwithſtanding he never
would receive any member of the Univerſity into his own Hall
without a *bene deceſſit*, and the conſent of the Head of the
College or Hall from whence he came.

† See Mr MIDDLETON's letter to the Biſhop of *Hereford*, in-
ſerted before the poſtſcript.

a long time before he was a member of the Univerfity? By what law did they who fat in judgment upon him pafs fentence againft him for an
act done fo long before he could poffibly be fubject
to their jurifdiction? Might he not with as much
equity have been punifhed for any thing he did
twenty years before? Let the advocates for this
fentence produce from all the annals of hiftory a
like cafe of defpotic proceeding in this nation!

But even fuppofing Mr V—C—— and his four
affeffors had not exceeded their power in this inftance, yet would any perfons of common huma-
nity and candor condemn a man, and turn him
out to ftarve, for one fingle ftep which was amifs,
when he acknowledged his error, and refolved to
avoid it for the future? Alas! if all were to be
dealt with upon fuch rigid principles, where
is the individual to be found, who is zealous and
earneft in any thing he undertakes, but may once
in his life at leaft, efpecially in the feafon of youth
and inexperience, act with rafhnefs and incon-
fideration?—It is well for us if even by our follies
we can learn wifdom *.

It

* Though Mr MIDDLETON's motive for this indifcretion of
preaching in a Chapel before he was ordained was pure and
difinterefted, yet I can produce an inftance of a like error in
which there does not appear quite fo much difinterefted love
for it.

The — alluded to happened about twenty years ago at
B——h in Shropfhire, where a certain gentleman, then unordained

I T may not be amifs here to fpeak a little concerning one of the charges againft Mr MATTHEWS,
namely, that he was refufed Ordination. The
reafon of which refufal, by the B—p of S——,
was, becaufe his Teftimonium was not figned by
his Tutor, owing I confefs (for I defire to fhew no
partiality) to Mr MATTHEWS's own neglect in de-
ferring to carry the Teftimonium to Mr. H——N in
proper time to have it figned and fent by the poft,
which occafioned him to inclofe it to the B———p
without Mr H——'s name; however, he added a
poftfcript to his Letter, fignifying that his Tutor
happened to be out, and that he hoped his Lordfhip would not object to the Teftimonium on account of its not being figned by him: But his
Lordfhip did object to it, and I think very juftly

C 2

too;

ordained, and of as low circumftances and extraction as any
of the expelled youths, but now a great Doctor in divinity,
affumed the character and habit of a clergyman, and mounting
the parifh pulpit in that town, took his text from *Eccles* iv.
11. " If two lie together then they have heat: but how can
" one be warm alone?" In what manner the gentleman
handled his fubject I was not particularly informed; but this is
certain, that he thereby fo much engaged the heart of a woman
who lived at the fign of the Pig and Caftle, and who had faved
upwards of one thoufand pounds, that fhe litterally refolved *to
lie alone* no longer, but kindly took our preacher to be her
hufband; from which circumftance his reverence, whofe real
name begins with B. is to this day called Doctor Pig and
Caftle, at ———— where he now refides. This anecdote I
had from a gentleman of undoubted veracity who lives upon
the fpot where our Hero held forth, and who knows him at
this inftant by the dignified title of Dr Pig and Caftle.

too; for although Mr M. had one Teftimonium
from the Principal of the Hall, and another figned
by three refpectable Clergymen, and authenticated
by the B—p of the Diocefs, yet that which he fent
to the B—p of S—— certainly ought to have been
figned by Mr H. the Vice-Principal, as it ran in
his name as much as in that of the Principal: not
to mention that the Teftimonium was by miftake of the B—p of —— who authenticated it,
directed to another Bifhop, inftead of the Bifhop
of S——. But his Lordfhip had ftill a more un-
furmountable objection againft Mr MATTHEWS,
for being what he deemed a Methodift; and accufed him of maintaining doctrines contrary to the
Church of *England*, and different from what he
(*viz.* his Lordfhip himfelf) held; to which Mr M.
replied, that he held no doctrines but what were
agreeable to the XXXIX Articles; and unlefs his
Lordfhip would be pleafed to fhew him wherein
they differed, he could not tell that they differed
at all: but this his Lordfhip declined, and gave
him to underftand that he was no ftranger to what
was going on at O——d. This then is the true
reafon why Mr MATTHEWS was refufed Ordination, and expelled the Univerfity, and not for
procuring a falfe Teftimonium, as was wickedly
reported, and inferted in the public papers, together with feveral other malicious untruths, in
order to prejudice the minds of people againft him
and the reft of the young men; fuch as " their
" preaching in the fields, in a barn, and on an
" oven,

"oven, as alfo attending the preaching of an old
"woman in an illicit conventicle: that one of
"them had been a Smith, and had fhoed the
"Tutor's horfe not long before. That fome of
"them had behaved with infolence and difobe-
"dience towards their Tutor." All which re-
ports were as falfe as GOD is true, and fhew what
fort of a caufe that muft be, which needs fuch
weapons in its defence. It is a fact indeed, that
one or two of thefe Gentlemen did leave the Hall
for a few nights without their Tutor's permiffion;
but it was upon fome urgent occafion, and he not
being in the way, they went to the Principal himfelf, as is ufual in fuch cafes, who gave them
leave to go.

THE next charge againft thefe young men to
be attended to, is, that they held heterodox doctrines, contrary to the Thirty-nine Articles of
the Church of *England*; and particularly, *that
they deny Free-will, or that good works are any part
of our Juftification: that they hold the doctrines of
Election and abfolute Predeftination, that whofoever
is once a child of* GOD, *is always a child of* GOD ;
*that we are juftified by Faith alone, and that the
influences of the Spirit are neceffary to conftitute every
one a child of* GOD.

"How is the gold become dim! how is the
"moft fine gold changed!"—Who could ever
have fuppofed that the famous U——y of O—d,
once

once the nurfing mother of fo many faithful fons
of the *Anglican* Church, fhould ever have expelled
her members for believing thofe very doctrines
which CRANMER and RIDLEY were martyred
within her walls for defending?—Who could ever
have believed that the heads of this ancient feat
of piety and learning fhould inflict a more fevere
punifhment upon her ftudents, for adhering to
the principles of the Reformation, than her fifter
Cambridge once did upon hers for denying them?
—Who could ever have imagined, that a folemn
fubfcription to Articles of Religion fhould be made
the teft of admiffion into an U——y, and yet a
ftedfaft belief of thofe very Articles, be made
the caufe of expulfion from the fame U——y?
And what furpaffes all the reft, that the very
perfons who are the inflicters of this moft igno-
minious fentence, fhould themfelves have fubfcribed and fworn to the defence of thofe Articles
over and over again, and are ready to fwear and
fubfcribe to them as many times more as prefer-
ment from one living to a better fhall be offered
them ; and notwithftanding they perfecute, even
to ftarving itfelf, thofe who really believe what
they fubfcribe to, are themfelves fed to the full
by fubfcribing to what they believe not a word
of; and whilft they would urge canonical difcipline for turning many found zealous Chriftians
out of the Church, are themfelves liable to be
excommunicated, *ipfo facto*, by the Vth Canon
of that very Church whereof they call themfelves
Minifters,

Minifters, and not to be reftored but by the Archbifhop, upon their repentance and revocation of
their wicked errors.

When light comes and bears hard upon darknefs,
it is an eafy matter to call it a libellous abufe of the
regular, dignified, orthodox Clergy ; and I doubt
not but when the faithful JEREMIAH cried out in
the fadnefs of his heart, *the Prophets prophefy falfly,
and the Priefts bear rule by their means, and my
people love to have it fo*; and that when ISAIAH by
the infpiration of the holy Ghoft called the paftors
of his day *blind watchmen and greedy dogs, which
could not bark, but loved to flumber, and only fought
after gain and ftrong liquor*; that their plain declarations had the fame conftruction put upon
them * : *Jer.* v. 31. *Ifa.* lvi. 10, 11, 12. But if
I prove the truth of every word I have afferted, then,
inftead of blaming me for bearing teftimony againft
the deluge of fin and error which has broken down
the walls of our *Sion,* who will not join with me
·in weeping fecretly *becaufe the enemy prevaileth,*
becaufe

---

* See alfo the xxxivth chapter of *Ezekiel*, which is full of
pathetical complaints againft the fhepherds of *Ifrael* for " eat-
" ing the fat and clothing themfelves with the wool, whilft
" they fed not the flock, neither healed that which was
" fick, nor bound up that which was broken, nor brought
" again that which was driven away, nor fought that which
" was loft."

because Jerusalem hath none to comfort her, all her friends have dealt treacherously with her; they are become her enemies? Lam. i. 2.

It is not my design to enter into a long defence of the doctrines before-mentioned : it will be am‑ply sufficient for the purpose in hand, if I prove beyond a doubt, that all the doctrines which these six students were expelled for maintaining, are the very fundamental avowed doctrines of the Church of *England*, and what they who passed the sentence have in the most sacred manner bound themselves to defend.

We will first speak of the doctrines of Free Agency, Election and Perseverance ; and as these hang so nearly one upon another, they may be considered under the same head.

One would think that whosoever reads the ninth tenth, and seventeenth Articles of our Church, cannot have the smallest doubt of the meaning of our Reformers who compiled them. The Ninth evidently sets forth the total corruption of every faculty of the soul by the fall of our first parents; the Tenth particularly declares the utter depravity of the natural will, which mani-fests itself in a continual bent to evil ; and the Seventeenth shews the free unchangeable love of GOD in choosing whom he will out of the lost children of ADAM, to make them partakers of

the

the great Salvation wrought out and perfected
by his fon JESUS CHRIST.

Thefe three Articles themfelves ftand as follows.

ARTICLE IX.

Of Original or Birth-Sin.

" Original Sin ftandeth not in the following
" of ADAM, (as the Pelagians do vainly talk;)
" but it is the faul̃t and corruption of the nature
" of every man, that naturally is ingendered of
" the offspring of ADAM, whereby man is very
" far gone from original righteoufnefs †, and is
" of his own nature inclined to evil, fo that the
" flefh lufteth always contrary to the Spirit; and
" therefore in every perfon born into this world,
" it deferveth GOD's wrath, and damnation.
" And this infection of nature doth remain, yea,
" in them that are regenerated ; whereby the luft
" of the flefh, called in Greek, φρονημα σαρκὸς,
" which fome do expound the *wifdom*, fome *fen-*
" *fuality*, fome the *affection*, fome the *defire* of
" the flefh, is not fubject to the law of GOD.
" And although there is no condemnation for
" them that believe and are baptized, yet the
" Apoftle doth confefs that concupifcence and
" luft hath of itfelf the nature of Sin."

ARTICLE

† *Quam longiffime,* as far as poffible.

ARTICLE X.

Of Free Will.

" The condition of man after the fall of ADAM,
" is fuch, that he cannot turn and prepare him-
" felf by his own natural ftrength and good works
" to faith and calling upon GOD : wherefore we
" have no power to do good works pleafant and
" acceptable to GOD without the grace of GOD
" by CHRIST preventing us, that we may have a
" good will, and working with us when we have
" that good will."

ARTICLE XVII.

Of Predeſtination and Election.

" Predeſtination to life is the everlaſting pur-
" pofe of GOD, whereby (before the foundations
" of the world were laid) he hath conſtantly de-
" creed by his counfel, fecret to us, to deliver
" from curfe and damnation thofe whom he hath
" chofen in CHRIST out of mankind, and to
" bring them by CHRIST to everlaſting Salvation,
" as veffels made to honor ; Wherefore they
" which be endued with fo excellent a benefit of
" GOD, be called according to GOD's purpofe
" by his Spirit working in due Seafon : they
" through grace obey the calling ; they be juſtified
" freely ; they be made fons of GOD by adoption ;
" they be made like the image of his only be-
" gotten

" gotten fon Jesus Christ; they walk religiously
" in good works, and at length, by God's mercy,
" they attain to everlasting felicity.

" As the godly confideration of Predeftination,
" and our Election in Christ, is full of fweet,
" pleafant, and unfpeakable comfort to godly
" perfons; and fuch as feel in themfelves the work-
" ing of the Spirit of Christ, mortifying the
" works of the flefh, and their earthly members,
" and drawing up their mind to high and heaven-
" ly things; as well becaufe it doth greatly
" eftablifh and confirm their faith of eternal Sal-
" vation, to be enjoyed through Christ, as
" becaufe it doth fervently kindle their love
" towards God: So for curious and carnal per-
" fons, lacking the Spirit of Christ, to have
" continually before their eyes the fentence of
" God's predeftination, is a moft dangerous
" downfal, whereby the devil doth thruft them
" either into defperation or into wretchlefsnefs
" of moft unclean living, no lefs perilous than
" defperation. Furthermore, we muft receive
" God's promifes in fuch wife, as they be gene-
" rally fet forth to us in holy fcripture. And
" in our doings, that will of God is to be followed
" which we have exprefly declared unto us in
" the Word of God."

Now when we confider that thefe Articles
were drawn up on purpofe to *prevent diverfity of
opinions* *,

opinions *, and therefore the compilers of them were particularly careful to avoid the poffibility of an ambiguous expreffion, and that the Declaration prefixed enjoins them to be taken in their plain *litteral grammatical fenfe, without being drawn afide any way,* and prohibits every *Clergyman, Head or Mafter of a College,* from putting *his own fenfe or comment upon any Article either in printing or preaching,* under pain of the royal difpleafure and the certain cenfure of the Church; I fay, when we confider this, it will not be an eafy matter to make the Ninth Article, which fets forth the total depravity of human nature, and the Tenth, which pofitively affirms that man fince the fall of ADAM has no free will nor power to do good works, or to turn, or even prepare himfelf to turn to GOD, harmonize with the fentiments of thofe *Heads* and *Mafters of Colleges,* who both in *printing* and *preaching* do vehemently infift upon it, that man, fince the fall of ADAM, hath both will and power to turn to GOD.

Equally difficult will it be to bring the opinions of thofe who have adopted the pride-foothing Arminian † herefy of univerfal Redemption,

to

* *Vide* the Declaration prefixed.

† When this fect of Arminians firft began to get footing in *England,* under the patronage of Archbifhop LAUD, one afking, " What do thefe Arminians hold ?" was anfwered to this effect ? " They already *hold* many good livings among us, " and it is likely they will foon *hold* all the fat benefices in the " Kingdom."

to correspond with the language of our Seventeenth Article, which in such plain terms afferts
that " Predeftination to life is the everlafting
" purpofe of God, whereby, before the founda-
" tions of the world were laid, he hath conftantly
" decreed by his counfel, fecret to us, to deliver
" from curfe and damnation thofe whom he hath
" chofen in CHRIST out of mankind, and to
" bring them by CHRIST to everlafting Salvation,
" as veffels made to honor."

Not lefs arduous muft be the tafk of thofe
Gentlemen who have folemnly fubfcribed to the
Eleventh Article, which affirms in exprefs words,
that we are juftified by Faith only, (of which I
fhall fpeak more fully under the next point of
doctrine) and neverthelefs would make us believe
they are found members and minifters of the
Church of *England*, whilft both in their words,
writings, and pulpit-harangues, to the great de-
rogation from the Redemption of JESUS CHRIST,
and the exaltation of fallen man, they are making Works a part of the finner's Juftification before GOD; and out of a mighty pretended zeal
for much more holinefs and morality than is ge-
nerally found in their own practice, are continually crying out againft this doctrine of our
Church, as a licentious doctrine and deftructive
of

" Kingdom."—It needed not a prophetic fpirit to foretel what
a rapid progrefs doctrines fo very pleafing to flefh and blood
would make.

of good Works, though the zealous exemplary lives of the maintainers of it, give daily and ample proof of the falfhood of the charge.

But as the certain fenfe of the Church of *England* touching her own Articles will be beft known by the cenfures which have been inflicted upon thofe who had fubfcribed to the truth of them, and afterwards *in writing or preaching* contradicted them; I proceed to give a fhort account of the cafe of the Rev. Mr BARRET, A. M. of *Caius* College, *Cambridge*, who in the thirty-feventh year of Queen ELIZABETH was fummoned before the Vicechancellor and Heads of Houfes in that Univerfity, for having, in a Sermon which he preached the 29th day of *April* 1595, before the faid Univerfity, broached divers pernicious errors contrary to the Articles of the Church of *England*; particularly, denying the doctrines of Affurance, Election, and Reprobation; and affirming, that a true child of GOD might finally and totally fall from grace. To which fummons the faid BARRET appeared; whereupon the Rev. Dr DUPORT, Vicechancellor of the Univerfity, with feven other Doctors in Divinity and Heads of Houfes, " en-
" tering into a mature deliberation, and diligently
" weighing and examining thefe pofitions, be-
" caufe it did manifeftly appear that the faid po-
" fitions were falfe, erroneous, and likewife *ma-*
" *nifeftly repugnant to the Religion received and*
" *eftablifhed in the Church of* England; adjudged
" and

" and declared, that the faid BARRET had incur-
" red the penalty of the forty-fifth Statute of that
" Univerfity, *De Concionibus* : and by vertue and
" tenor of that Statute they decreed and adjudged
" the faid BARRET to make a public recantation,
" in fuch words and form as fhould be prefcribed
" unto him by the Vicechancellor and the Heads,
" or upon his refufal to be *perpetually expelled*
" from the Univerfity : binding him likewife in
" an affumpfit of forty pounds to appear perfon-
" ally upon two days warning before the faid
" Vicechancellor or his Deputy, at what time and
" place they fhould require.—Afterwards this
" BARRET was refummoned before the Vice-
" chancellor, Dr GOADE, Dr TYNDALL, Dr
" BARWELL, and Dr PRESTON, who delivered
" him the Recantation in writing, admonifhing
" and peremptorily enjoining him on *Saturday*
" following, being the 10th of *May*, immediately
" after the Clerum ended, to go up in perfon
" into St *Mary*'s pulpit, where he had publifhed
" thefe errors, and there openly in the face of the
" Univerfity to read and make this Recantation ;
" which he did accordingly, though not with
" that humility which was expected.—Not long
" after this, to fhew that thefe pofitions are but a
" bridge to Popery, Mafter BARRET departed
" the Univerfity, and went beyond fea, where he
" turned a profeffed Papift ; but came back to
" *England*, where he lived a Layman's life, and
                                        " becam

" became an open, dangerous, violent, and moſt
" pernicious ſeducing Papiſt."

See the learned Mr P<small>RYNNE</small>'s
Anti-Arminianiſm, p. 61. 2d edit.

For the Recantation itſelf, Mr P<small>RYNNE</small> tells
us, it was fairly printed and publiſhed in Queen
E<small>LIZABETH</small>'s days, in the very ſame words
that he has given it to his readers; and that he
himſelf had a tranſcript of it in Latin, taken out
of an original copy in B<small>ARRET</small>'s own hand, which
agrees verbatim with the Engliſh one, except that
in the Latin copy the ſeventeenth Article is in-
ſerted at length. I ſhall therefore write out this
Recantation as it ſtands recorded by Mr P<small>RYNNE</small>;
and for the benefit of the unlearned, and to avoid
prolixity, ſhall only tranſcribe the Engliſh copy,
referring thoſe who are deſirous to ſee the Latin
one to Mr P<small>RYNNE</small>'s book.

A Copie of a Recantation of certaine Errors
raked out of the Dunghill of Poperie &
Pelagianiſme, publiquely made by Maſter
B<small>ARRET</small> of <i>Kayes</i> Colledge in <i>Cambridge</i>,
the 10th of <i>May</i>, in this preſent yeere of
our L<small>ORD</small>, 1595, in the Univerſitie Church
called St M<small>ARIES</small> in <i>Cambridge</i>; which
Errors he (together with Mr H<small>ARSNET</small> of
Pembroke Hall *) did raſhly hold and
maintaine. Tranſlated out of Latine into
Engliſh.

" PREACH-

* It is reaſonable to ſuppoſe from the mention of theſe two
Gentlemen, that no others in the Univerſity were ſuſpected of
maintaining the like errors. Now, alas, their name is <i>Legion</i>.

" PREACHING in Latin not long fince
" in the Univerfity Church (right worfhipfull)
" many things flipped from me both falfely and
" rafhly fpoken, whereby I underftand the minds
" of many have been grieved; to the end therefore
" that I may fatisfie the Church, and the Truth
" which I have publiquely hurt, I doe make
" this publique confeffion, both repeating and
" revoking my Errors.

Firft, " I faid that no man in this tranfitory
" world is fo ftrongly underpropped, at leaft by
" the certainety of faith, that is, unlefs (as I af-
" terwards expounded it) by Revelation*, that
" he ought to be affured of his owne Salvation.
" But now I proteft before GOD, and acknow-
" ledge in my confcience, that they which are
" juftified by faith, have peace towards GOD,
" that is, have reconciliation with GOD, and doe
" ftand in that grace by faith : therefore that
" they ought to be certaine, and affured of their
" owne Salvation, even by the certainety of faith
" itfelf."

Secondly, " I affirmed that the faith of PETER
" could not fail, but that other mens faith may :
" for (as I then faid) our LORD prayed not for
" the faith of every particular man. But now
" being of a better, and more found judgement,

D (according

---

* This denial of Affurance, except by immediate Revela-
tion, is the very Doctrine of the Council of *Trent*, and a main
pillar of Popery.

" (according to that which CHRIST teacheth in
" plain words, *John* xvii. 20. *I pray not for thefe*
" *alone,* (that is the Apoftles) *but for them alfo*
" *which fhall beleeve in me through their word* ;) I
" acknowledge that CHRIST did pray for the
" faith of every particular beleever, and that by
" the Vertue of that praier of CHRIST, every true
" beleever is fo ftaied up, that his faith cannot
" faile."

Thirdly, " Touching perfeverance unto the
" end, I faid, that *that* certainty concerning the
" time to come, is proude, forafmuch as it is in
" it's owne nature contingent of what kind the
" perfeverance of every man is : neither did I
" affirme it to be proude only, but to be moft
" wicked. But now I freely proteft, that the
" true and juftifying Faith (whereby the faithfull
" are moft neerely united unto CHRIST,) is fo
" firme, as alfo for the time to come fo certaine,
" that it can never be rooted up out of the minds
" of the faithfull by any tentations of the flefh,
" the world, or the devill himfelf. So that he
" that once hath this faith, fhall ever have it :
" for by the benefit of that juftifying faith CHRIST
" dwelleth in us, and we in CHRIST ; therefore
" it cannot but bee both increafed, (CHRIST
" growing in us daily,) as alfo perfevere unto the
" end, becaufe GOD doeth give conftancy."

Fourthly,

(51)

Fourthly, " I affirmed that there was no dif-
" tinction in faith; but in the perfons beleeving:
" In which I confefse that I did erre : now I freely
" acknowledge, that temporary faith (which as
" BERNARD witneffeth is therefore fained, becaufe
" it is temporary,) is diftinguifhed, and differeth
" from that faving faith whereby finners appre-
" hending CHRIST are juftified before GOD for
" ever; not in meafure and degrees, but in the
" very thing itfelfe. Moreover I adde, that
" JAMES doth make mention of a dead faith,
" and PAUL of a faith that worketh by love."

Fifthly, " I added, that forgivenefse of finnes
" is an Article of faith, but not particular, nei-
" ther belonging to this man, nor to that man ;
" that is, (as I expounded) that no true faithfull
" man, either can, or ought, certainely to beleeve
" that his finnes are forgiven. But now I am of
" another minde, and doe freely confefs, that
" every true faithfull man is bound by this Ar-
" ticle of faith, (to wit, I beleeve the forgivenefse
" of finnes,) certainely to beleeve that his owne
" particular finnes are freely forgiven him ; nei-
" ther doth it follow hereupon, that that petition
" of the LORD's prayer (to wit, forgive us our
" trefpaffes, is needlefs ; for in that petition,
" we afke not only the gift, but alfo the increafe
" of faith."

Sixthly,

Sixthly, " Thefe words efcaped me in my Ser-
" mon, *viz.* As for thofe that are not faved, I
" doe moft ftrongly beleeve, and doe freely pro-
" teft that I am fo perfwaded againft CALVIN,
" PETER MARTYR, and the reft, that finne is
" the true, proper, and firft caufe of Reproba-
" tion. But now being better inftructed ; I fay,
" that the Reprobation of the wicked is from
" everlafting; and that that faying of AUGUS-
" TINE to SIMPLICIAN is moft true, *viz.* if finne
" were the caufe of Reprobation, then no man
" fhould be elected, becaufe GOD doeth foreknow
" all men to be defiled with it, and (that I may
" fpeak freely,) I am of the fame minde ; and
" do beleeve concerning the doctrine of Election,
" and Reprobation, AS THE CHURCH OF ENGLAND
" BELEEVETH, AND TEACHETH IN THE BOOKE OF
" THE ARTICLES OF FAITH, IN THE ARTICLE
" OF PREDESTINATION."

Laft of all, " I uttered thefe words rafhly
" againft CALVIN, a man that hath very well
" deferved of the Church of GOD ; to wit, that
" he durft prefume to lift up himfelfe above the
" high and almighty GOD. By which words I
" confefse, that I have done great injury to that
" moft learned and right godly man : And I doe
" moft humbly befeech you all, to pardon this
" my rafhnefse ; as alfo in that I have uttered
" many

" many bitter words agaiuft Peter Martyr †,
" TheodoreBeza, JeromeZanchius, Francis
" Junius, and the reft of the fame religion, be-
" ing the lights and ornaments of our Church ;
" calling them by the odious names of Caluinifts,
" and other fcandalous termes ; branding them
" with a moft grievious mark of reproach : whom
" becaufe our Church doth worthily reverence,
" it was not meet, that I fhould take away their
" good name from them, or any way impaire
" their credit, or dehort others of our countrymen
" from reading their moft learned workes. I am
" therefore very forry, and grieved for this moft
" grievious offence, which I have publickely
" given to this moft famous Univerfity, which
" is the Temple of true religion, and facred re-
" ceptable of piety : And I doe promife that (by
" God's helpe,) I will never hereafter offend in
" the like fort : and I doe earneftly befeech you
" (right worfhipfull,) and all others to whom I
" have given this offence, either in the former
" Articles, or in any part of my faid fermon, that
" you would of your courtefy pardon me, upon
" this my repentance."

Mr Prynne faith, that whatever he has afferted concerning this affair of Barret, was col-

lected

---

† Peter Martyr, being invited into England by King
Edward the fixth, was made Divinity Profeffor in the Univerfity of Oxford, and was a zealous promoter of the Reformation.

lected out of the original order for his recantation made by the heads of the University of *Cambridge*, and there recorded in the University-regifter for the benefit of pofterity ; the tranfcript of which order he has inferted at large, not only becaufe it is an invincible evidence of our anti-arminian points in queftion, but becaufe he was informed that fince his tranfcript that order had been razed out of the Univerfity-regifter by fome well-wifhers to BARRET's herefies.

The maintaining of thefe doctrines by BARRET and one PETER BARO, a Frenchman, Lady *Margaret*'s Profeffor in that Univerfity (who, by the bye, is not the laft Lady *Margaret*'s Profeffor who has imbibed the fame errors) gave rife to what are ufually called the *Lambeth Articles*, which were compofed and approved at the palace at *Lambeth*, by the Archbifhops of *Canterbury* and *York*, the Bifhops of *London* and *Bangor*, and fundry other eminent Divines, and by them fent to *Cambridge*, (where they were highly approved by the whole Univerfity) to compofe the differences which had arifen.

As thefe nine Articles were drawn up by the greateft men of our Church, and received by the faid Univerfity as containing the undoubted fenfe of the Anglican Church in the points of Election, Perfeverance, Free-will, Affurance, Saving Faith, Efficacious

Efficacious Grace, &c. I shall now insert them both in Latin and English.

1. *Deus ab æterno prædestinavit quosdam ad vitam ; quosdam reprobavit ad mortem.*

1. GOD from eternity hath predestinated certain men unto life ; certain men he hath reprobated unto death.

2. *Causa movens aut efficiens prædestinationis ad vitam, non est prævisio fidei, aut perseverantiæ, aut bonorum operum, aut ullius rei quæ insit in personis prædestinatis, sed sola voluntas beneplaciti Dei.*

2. The moving, or efficient cause of predestination unto life, is not the foresight of faith, or of perseverance, or of good workes, or of any thing that is in the persons predestinated, but only the good will and pleasure of GOD.

3. *Prædestinatorum præfinitus & certus est numerus, qui nec augeri, nec minui possit.*

3. There is a predetermined, and certain number of the predestinate, which can neither be augmented nor diminished.

4. *Qui non sunt prædestinati ad salutem, necessario propter peccata sua damnabuntur.*

4. They who are not predestinated to salvation, shall be necessarily damned for their sins.

5. *Vera, viva, & justificans fides, & spiritus Dei justificantis, non extinguitur, non excidit, non evanescit in electis, aut finaliter, aut totaliter.*

D 4   5 A

5. A true, living, and juſtifying faith, and the Spirit of God juſtifying, is not extinguiſhed, it falleth not away, it vaniſheth not away in the elect either finally or totally.

6. Homo vére fidelis, id eſt, fide juſtificante præditus, certus eſt plerophoria fidei, de remiſſione peccatorum ſuorum, & ſalute ſempiterna ſua per Chriſtum.

6. A man truly faithful, that is, ſuch a one who is endued with a juſtifying faith, is certain with a full aſſurance of faith of the remiſſion of ſins, and his everlaſting ſalvation by Chriſt.

7. Gratia ſalutaris non tribuitur, communicatur, non conceditur univerſis hominibus, qua ſervari poſſint.

7. Saving grace is not given, is not communicated, is not granted to all men, by which they may be ſaved.

8. Nemo poteſt venire ad Chriſtum, niſi datum ei fuerit, & niſi Pater eum traxerit ; & omnes homines non trabuntur a Patre ut veniat ad Filium.

8. No man can come unto Chriſt, unleſs it ſhall be given unto him, and unleſs the Father ſhall draw him; and all men are not drawn by the Father, that they may come to the Son.

9. Non eſt poſitum in arbitrio, aut poteſtate uniuscujuſque hominis ſervari.

9. It is not in the will or power of every one to be ſaved.

IN

I N many of the old Bibles, particularly in that called the Bifhop's Bible, the only one in ufe in Queen ELIZABETH's time, are Queftions and Anfwers touching the doctrine of Predeftination, which, by order of the faid godly Bifhops, were bound up with the fame Bible: As thefe queftions and anfwers are not only very excellent in them-felves, but clearly demonftrate the fenfe of our Church touching the doctrines in queftion, I fhall infert them at large.

Certaine Queftions and Anfwers touching the Doctrine of Predeftination; printed by ROBERT BARKER, *anno* 1607, which were then bound up, and fold with our Englifh Bibles.

Queftion. Why doe men fo much vary in mat-ters of Religion?

Anfwer. Becaufe all have not the like meafure of knowledge, neither doe all beleeve the Gofpel of CHRIST.

Queft. What is the reafon thereof?

Anfw. Becaufe they onely beleeve the Gofpel and Doctrine of CHRIST, which are ordained unto eternall life.

Qu. Are not all ordained to eternall life?

An. Some are veffels of wrath ordained unto deftruction, as others are veffels of mercy pre-pared to glory.

Qu. How ftandeth it with GOD's juftice, that fome are appointed to damnation?

An.

An. Very well; becaufe all men have in themfelves finne, which deferveth no leffe, and therefore the mercy of God is wonderfull in that he vouchfafed to fave fome of that finneful race, and to bring them to the knowledge of the truth.

Qu. If God's ordinance and determination muft of neceffity take effect, then what need any man to care ; for he that liveth well, muft needes be damned, if he be thereunto ordained ; and he that liveth ill muft needes be faved, if he be thereunto appointed.

An. Not fo : for it is not poffible, that either the Elect fhould alwaies be without care to doe well, or that the Reprobate fhould have any will thereunto. For to have either good will or good workes, is a teftimony of the Spirit of God, which is given to the Elect onely, whereby faith is fo wrought in them, that being grafted into Christ, they grow in holineffe to that glory whereunto they are appointed. Neither are they fo vaine as once to thinke that they may doe as they lift themfelves, becaufe they are predeftinated unto falvation ; but rather they endeavour to walke in fuch good works as God in Christ Jesus hath ordained them unto, and prepared for them to be occupied in, to their owne comfort, ftay and affurance, and to his glory.

Qu. But how fhall I know my felfe to be one of thofe whom God hath ordained to life eternall ?

An. By the motions of fpirituall life, which belongeth onely to the children of God ; by the
which

which that life is perceived, even as the life of
the body is defcerned by the fenfe and motions
thereof.

. Qu. What meane you by the motions of fpirituall life?

, ; *An.* I meane remorfe of confcience, joined with
the loathing of finne, and the love of righteouf-
nefse ; the hand of faith reaching unto life eternall
in CHRIST, the confcience comforted in diftrefse,
and raifed up to confidence in GOD by the worke
of his fpirit : A thankfull remembrance of GOD's
benefits received, and the ufing of all adverfities
as occafion of amendment fent from GOD.

Qu. Cannot fuch perifh as at fome time or
other feele thefe motions within themfelves?

. *An.* It is not poffible that they fhould : For
as GOD's purpofe is not changeable, fo he repent-
eth not of the gifts and graces of his adoption :
NEITHER DOTH HE CAST OFF THOSE WHOM HE
HATH ONCE RECEIVED.

Qu. Why then fhould we pray by the example of DAVID, that he caft us not from his face,
and that he take not his holy Spirit from us?

An. In fo praying we make proteftation of the
weaknefs of the flefh, which moveth us to doubt:
Yet fhould we not have courage to afke, if we were
not affured that GOD will give, according to his
purpofe and promife, that which we require.

Qu. Doe the children of GOD feele the motions aforefaid alwaies alike?

An.

An. No truely : for God fometimes, to prove his, feemeth to leave them in fuch fort, that the flefh overmatcheth the fpirit, whereof arifeth trouble of confcience. for the time ; yet the Spirit of adoption is never taken from them that have once received it ; elfe might they perifh : but as in many difeafes of the body, the powers of the bodily life are letted : fo in fome affaults the motions of fpiritual life are not perceived, becaufe they lie hidden in our manifold infirmities, as the fire covered with afhes. Yet as after ficknefle commeth health, and after clouds the fun fhineth cleare ; fo the powers of fpirituall life will more or lefse be felt and perceived in the children of God.

Qu. What if I never feele thefe motions in myfelfe, fhall I defpaire, and thinke myfelfe caft away ?

An. God forbid : for God calleth his, at what time he feeth good ; and the inftruments whereby he ufually calleth, have not the like effect at all times ; yet is it not good to neglect the means whereby God hath determined to worke the falvation of his. For as wax is not melted without heate, nor clay hardened but by means thereof ; fo God ufeth means both to draw thefe unto himfelfe, whom he hath appointed unto falvation : And alfo to bewray the wickednefse of them whom he juftly condemneth.

Qu. By

Qu. By what meanes ufeth GOD to draw men to himfelfe that they may be faved ?

An. By the preaching of his word, and the miniftring of his facraments thereunto annexed, &c.

These Queftions and Anfwers concerning Predeftination, which are full and punctual to our purpofe, were always printed at the end of the old Teftament, and bound up and fold, *cum privilegio*, with this authorized tranflation of the Bible, till about the Year 1615, fince which no Bibles of this fort were printed. We may therefore ufe them as a pregnant teftimony, a punctual declaration of the doctrine of our Church.

To thefe authorities may be added the Catechifm, drawn up by the Right Rev. Father in GOD JOHN PONET, Bifhop of *Winchefter*, which was fet forth by command of King EDWARD the Sixth for all fchoolmafters to teach. Though the whole of it is an excellent compendium of chriftian divinity, yet in order to be as brief as poffible, I fhall only quote from it the following paffage, which will clearly fhew the fenfe of our Reformers, and of the original, pure, primitive Church of *England* in fome points of doctrine, which are now looked upon as by far too abfurd to be fubmitted to by the wifdom of this enlightened age.

———" As

⌐——⌐" As many as are in the true faith ſtedfaſt,
" were fore-choſen, predeſtinated, and appointed
" to everlaſting life before the world was made,
" witneſſe hereof they have within their hearts,
" the ſpirit of CHRIST, the author, earneſt, and
" unfailable pleadge of their faith : which faith
" only is able to perceive the myſteries of GOD :
" only brings peace unto the heart : only taketh
" hold on the righteouſneſs that is in CHRIST
" JESUS."

Maſter. " Doth then the Spirit alone, and
" faith (ſleepe we never ſo ſecurely, or ſtand we
" never ſo rechleſſe or ſlothfull) ſo worke all
" things for us, as without any helpe of our owne
" to carry us idle up to heaven ?

Schol. " I uſe Maſter (as you have taught me)
" to make a difference between the cauſe and the
" effect. The firſt principall and moſt proper
" cauſe of our juſtification and ſalvation, is the
" goodneſs and love of GOD. Whereby HE CHOSE
" US FOR HIS, BEFORE HE MADE THE WORLD.
" After that, GOD granteth us to be called by
" the preaching of the goſpel of JESUS CHRIST,
" when the Spirit of the LORD is powered into
" us, by whoſe guiding and governance we be led
" to ſettle our truſt in GOD, and hope for the
" performance of his promiſe. With this choice
" is joined as a companion, the mortifying of the
" olde man, that is, of our affection and luſt.
" From the ſame Spirit alſo cometh our ſanctifi-
                                        " cation,

" cation, the love of GOD, and of our neigh-
" bour, juſtice and uprightneſs of life: Finally,
" to ſay all in ſumme, whatever is in us or may
" be done of us, honeſt, pure, true, and good,
" that altogether ſpringeth out of this moſt plea-
" ſant rock : from this moſt plentiful fountaine,
" the goodneſs, love, choiſe, and unchangeable
" purpoſe of GOD ; he is the cauſe, the reſt are
" the fruits and effects. Yet are alſo the good-
" neſſe, choiſe, and Spirit of GOD, and CHRIST
" himſelfe, cauſes conjoyned and coupled each
" with other : which may be reckoned among
" the principal cauſes of Salvation. As oft there-
" fore as we uſed to ſay, that we are made righ-
" teous and SAVED BY FAITH ONLY ; it is meant
" thereby, that Faith, or rather truſt alone, doth
" lay hand upon, underſtand and perceive our
" righteous making to be given us of GOD freely;
" that is to ſay, by no deſerts of our owne, but
" by the free grace of the almighty Father;
" moreover Faith doth ingender into us love of
" our neighbour, and ſuch works as GOD is pleaſed
" withal. For if it be a lively and true Faith,
" quickned by the Holy Ghoſt, ſhe is the mo-
" ther of all good ſaying and doing. By this ſhort
" tale it is evident, whence, and by what meanes
" we attaine to be righteous. For not by the
" worthineſſe of our deſerving were we heretofore
" choſen, or long agoe ſaved, but by the only
" mercy of GOD and pure grace of CHRIST our
" LORD ;

" Lord; whereby we were in him made to doë
" thefe good workes that God had appointed for
" us to walk in. And although good workes can-
" not deferve to make us righteous before God,
" yet doe they fo cleave unto faith, that neither
" faith can be found without them, nor good
" workes be any where found without faith."

We will bring yet another proof that the doctrine
of man's merits, and his free will to good or evil,
were held in utter abhorrence by our Reformers,
yea fo much, that they even call them *doctrines of
devils*, and rank them with the Mafs, Purgatory,
Prayers for the Dead, and fuch like limbs of
Antichrift; and that the doctrines of Free-grace,
Election, and Perfeverance, are the ancient, undoubted, received tenets of the Church of *England*; and this fhall be from the Prayers and truly
excellent Confeffion of Faith bound up with the
old Common-Prayer-Books and Bibles, from
whence I extract verbatim what follows.

" I believe and confefs one holy Church, which
" Church is not feen to man's eye, but only
" known to God; who of the loft fons of Adam
" hath ordained fome as veffels of wrath to dam-
" nation, and hath chofen others as veffels of his
" mercy to be faved; the which in due time he
" calleth to integrity of life, and godly conver-
" fation, to make them a glorious Church in
" himfelf, &c. &c.

So

So again—" The defence of Christ's Church
" appertaineth to Chriſtian Magiſtrates againſt
" all Idolaters and Hereticks, as Papiſts, Ana-
" baptiſts *, with ſuch like limbs of antichriſt,
" to root out all doctrines of devils and men;
" as the Maſs, Purgatory, Limbus patrum,
" Prayers to Saints, and for the Dead, Free-
" will, diſtinction of Meats, Apparel, and
" Days; Vows of ſingle Life; preſence at Idol-
" ſervice, Man's merits, with ſuch like;
" which draw us from the ſociety of Christ's
" Church, wherein ſtandeth only remiſſion of
" ſins purchaſed by Christ's blood to all them
" that believe, whether they be Jews or Gentiles,
" and lead us to a vain confidence in creatures,
" and truſt in our own imaginations; the puniſh-
" ment whereof, although God oftentimes de-
" ferreth in this life, yet after the reſurrection,
" when our ſouls and bodies ſhall riſe again to
" immortality, they shall be damned with
" unquenchable fire : and then we, which
" have forſaken all men's wiſdom to cleave to
" Christ, ſhall hear the joyful voice of, *Come
" ye bleſſed of my Father,*" &c. &c.

One of the Prayers formerly and ſtill printed
at the end of moſt Bibles and Common-Prayer
Books, begins with theſe words, " Honour and
" praiſe be given unto thee, O Lord God
" Almighty, moſt dear Father of heaven, for all

E thy

* Theſe Anabaptiſts were very different from thoſe we now call Baptiſts.

" thy mercies and loving-kindnefs fhewed unto
" us, in that it hath pleafed thy gracious good-
" nefs freely and of thine own accord to elect
" and choofe us unto falvation before the begin-
" ning of the world," &c. &c. &c.

I might bring proof upon proof from the various Offices of the Church of *England*, from the
Liturgy *, Catechifm †, Homilies §, Office of
Baptifm ‖, and Burial of the Dead **, &c. to demonftrate

* Make thy *chofen* people joyful. O God, who haft knit
together the *Elect* in one communion, &c.

† In God the Holy Ghoft, who fanctifieth me and all the
Elect people of God.

§ The Scripture doth acknowledge but two places after this
life ; *the one proper to the* ELECT *and bleffed of* God, *the other
to the* REPROBATE, &c.

‖ Almighty God, &c. grant that all thy fervants which fhall
be baptized in this water may receive the fullnefs of thy grace,
and ever remain in the number of *thy* faithful and *Elect*
children.

** " That it may pleafe thee of thy gracious goodnefs
" fhortly to accomplifh the number of thine Elect."—" Al-
" mighty God, with whom do live the fpirits of them who
" depart hence in the Lord, and in whom the fouls of them
" *that be elected*, after they be delivered from the burden of
" flefh, be in joy and felicity.' —This prayer is expunged out of
all the Common-Prayer Books which have been printed of late
years 'tis a prayer originally made for the Queen, wherein
were the following words " Almighty God, who haft pro-
" mifed to be the Father of thine *Elect* and of their feed,"
&c. in the old Common-Prayer Books, at the end of
the .... , from which I extract the following .... Almighty and merciful Lord,
which givet unto thy holier people the Holy Ghoft as a
fure

monſtrate that the doƈtrines before mentioned, and
which the young men were expelled the Univerſity for holding, are the pure, avowed, fundamental doƈtrines of that Church; and that where
we find any expreſſions in her Service, &c. of
CHRIST dying for *all* men, having redeemed *all*
mankind, and being a propitiation for the ſins of
the world; theſe mean, that his ſacrifice and undertaking were infinite and all-ſufficient, he being
the very and eternal GOD; which if he were not,
ſin having an eternal demerit, no fleſh living could
have been ſaved: But the application of this ſacrifice and undertaking is every where confined to
the Eleƈt people of GOD, to his ſheep, his choſen,
his church, his ſeed, his ſpouſe, his members; to
thoſe whom the Father hath given him out of the
world: I ſay, I might bring proof upon proof of
this, but let the authorities already produced ſuf-
fice to cloſe the point in hand; which I have
dwelt the longer upon, becauſe of all others, the
doƈtrines which deny fallen man's free will to
good, and which maintain an abſolute choice of
ſome in preference to others (" even before the
" children are born or have done good or evil,
" that the purpoſe of GOD according to Eleƈtion
" may ſtand, not of works, but of him that

E 2   " calleth)

ſure pledge of thy heavenly kingdom, grant unto us this holy
Spirit, that he may bear witneſs with our Spirits that we be
thy children and heirs of thy kingdom; and that by the opera-
tions of this Spirit, we may kill all carnal luſts, &c.

" calleth *") are moſt hateful to the natural pride of our hearrts, which will be ever taking up the language of St Paul's Objector, and ſaying, " Why doth he yet find fault, for who hath re- " ſiſted his will?" (for to this one cavil all the reaſonings and reaſoners againſt this doctrine do at laſt come, if they could reaſon an hundred years together:) But as St Augustine, ſpeaking of this point, obſerves, the only reply of thoſe who wiſh not to be wiſer than the Apoſtle, will be, " Nay, but, O man, who art thou that replieſt " againſt God? Shall the thing formed ſay to him " that formed it, Why haſt thou made me thus? ", Hath not the potter power over the clay, of " the ſame lump to make one veſſel unto honor, " and another unto diſhonor?" A reply which it is evident that St Paul could not have made without a glaring abſurdity, if the Election he ſpoke of, as ſome pretend, was only a general outward calling of whole nations to the Chriſtian Faith.

We will cloſe this head with the determination of the famous Proteſtant Synod of *Dort*, held *anno* 1619, to which five Biſhops and Doctors in divinity were ſent by King James I. as Repreſentatives of the *Engliſh* Church, where the doctrines of Free-will, Univerſal Redemption, and Falling from Grace, were condemned by all the Reformed Churches, as being the ſpawn of Popery and Pelagianiſm, repugnant

to

* Rom. ix. 11.

to Scripture, and the freedom of God's Grace; and the chief abettors of thefe errors were de- prived and debarred by this Synod from all ec- clefiaftical Functions, and FROM ALL OFFICES IN ANY UNIVERSITY, till they had openly repented and recanted their errors. And in the fucceeding reign, the honorable Houfe of Commons did move his Majefty to put away from his prefence fuch of his Chaplains as there was caufe to be- lieve were infected with Arminian doctrines. But how far this faction has fince prevailed towards the overthrow of the Church, dreadful experience fhews *.

ANOTHER point of doctrine, and that of the greateft importance, comes now to be treated of; viz. Juftification by Faith alone, without Works: In handling of which it is only confiftent with my defign to prove that this is the plain, indubitable, received doctrine of the Church of England: and if I make this fully appear, then what are we to think of thofe great and learned Rabbies who are advanced to the higheft dignities in that Church by fubfcribing to this doctrine, and

E 3   yet

* The learned Dr EDWARDS, in his *Veritas Redux*, brings a quotation from ARMINIUS himfelf, to prove that he never held that a true child of GOD could fall from Grace : and it is well known, that the faid ARMINIUS allowed Juftification to be by Faith alone. How much beyond their Mafter do our modern Arminians go, and what need have we to be on our guard againft fuch turbulent, unquiet fpirits, as the Synod of *Dort* calls them !

yet fpeak againſt it, write againſt it, preach againſt
it, yea, and expel thoſe who having ſubſcribed to
it at their Matriculation, and being obliged to ſub-
ſcribe to it again at their Ordination, do firmly
believe the truth of it, and dare not from any lu-
crative motives *follow a multitude to do evil.*

We will firſt conſider the Eleventh Article of
our Church, which runs as follows.

Of the *Juſtification* of *Man.*

" We are accounted righteous before GOD
" ONLY for the merit of our LORD and Saviour
" JESUS CHRIST, by faith, and not for our own
" works or deſervings. Wherefore that we are
" JUSTIFIED BY FAITH ONLY, is a moſt
" wholeſome doctrine, and very full of comfort,
" as more largely is expreſſed in the Homily of
" Juſtification."

Words cannot be plainer than thoſe of this Article ; I ſhall not therefore darken it by any comment ; but let the Homily to which it refers ſpeak
the ſenſe in which both the Article itſelf and that
Homily are clearly to be taken.

From the Homily I extract what follows.

" The Apoſtle toucheth ſpecially three things
" which muſt go together in our Juſtification.
" Upon GOD's part, his great mercy and grace.
" Upon CHRIST's part, juſtice, that is, the Satis-
" faction of GOD's juſtice, or the price of our
" Redemption by the offering of his body and
                                            " ſhedding

" shedding of his blood, with fulfilling of the
" Law perfectly and thoroughly ; and upon our
" part true and lively Faith in the merits of Jesus
" Christ, which yet is not ours, but by God's
" working in us."

Here is no mention of works either as conditions or as parts of Justification, which, as plain as words can make it, is attributed only to Faith ; and even that Faith not our own, but God's working in us.—So also in the third part of the Homily of Salvation, we read, " And forasmuch as it is all one sentence in effect to say,
" Faith without Works, and only Faith doth
" justify us ; therefore the old ancient fathers of
" the Church, from time to time, have uttered
" our Justification with this speech, *Only faith justifieth us* ;" meaning no other thing than St
Paul meant, when he said, " Faith without
" works justifieth us."—And in another place :
" The sum of all Paul's disputation is this, That
" if justice come of Works, then it cometh not
" of Grace ; and if it come of Grace, then it cometh not of Works. And to this end tend all the
" Prophets, as St Peter saith in the tenth of the
" *Acts*, of Christ all the Prophets do witness, that
" through his name, all they that believe in him
" shall receive the remission of sins. And after this
" wise, to be justified *only* by this true and lively
" Faith in Christ ; speak all the old and antient
" authors, both Greeks and Latins ; of whom I
" will especially rehearse three, Hilary, Basil,

E 4   " and

" and AMBROSE: St HILARY faith thefe words
" plainly in the ninth Canon upon MATTHEW,
" Faith only juftifieth." And St BASIL, a Greek
" author, writeth thus; This is a perfect and
" whole rejoicing in GOD, when a man advanceth
" not himfelf for his own righteoufnefs, but ac-
" knowledgeth himfelf to lack true juftice and
" righteoufnefs, and to be juftified by the only
" Faith in CHRIST." And PAUL (faith he) " doth
" glory in the contempt of his own righteoufnefs,
" and that he looketh for the righteoufnefs of
" GOD, by Faith." Thefe be the very words of
" St BASIL : and St AMBROSE, a Latin author, faith
" thefe words ; This is the ordinance of GOD,
" that they which believe in CHRIST fhould be
" faved without Works, by Faith only, freely
" receiving remiffion of their fins." Confider
" diligently thefe words, WITHOUT WORKS, BY
" FAITH ONLY, FREELY WE RECEIVE REMISSION
" OF OUR SINS." What can be fpoken more plain-
" ly, than to fay, that freely without Works, by
" Faith only, we obtain remiffion of our fins ?
" Thefe and other like fentences, that we be jufti-
" fied by Faith only, freely and without Works,
" we do read oftentimes in the beft and moft
" ancient writers. As befide HILARY, BASIL
" and St AMBROSE before rehearfed, we read the
" fame in ORIGEN, St CHRYSOSTOM, St CYPRI-
" AN, St AUGUSTINE, PROSPER, OECUMENIUS,
" PROCLUS, BERNARDUS, ANSELM, and many
                                          " other

" other authors Greek and Latin." Thus far our Homily.

Now are thefe the very words of our Church? What a different found then do thofe trumpets give (O pleafing mufic to the Popifh ear!) which make fo much noife about Works being parts of or conditions of our Juftification? And whilft in words fome of them deny that they maintain the doctrine of man's merit, are, in fact, teaching him to look to a righteoufnefs of his own, made up of terms, qualifications, conditions, &c. for acceptance before God, and all this under the dreadful apprehenfions of fapping the foundation of good Works *. But certain it is, that whofoever thinks to build good Works upon any other foundation than that of Faith in CHRIST, will be found building upon the fand : for if the Church of *England* be in the right, Works are fo far from being a condition of Juftification, that we cannot do a good Work till we are juftified ; but all our

Works

---

* " It is a childifh cavil (faith the judicious HOOKER, in his
" treatife on Juftification) which our adverfaries fo greatly
" pleafe themfelves with, exclaiming, that we tread all Chriftian
" Virtues under our feet, becaufe we teach, that Faith alone
" juftifieth. Whereas by this fpeech we never meant to ex-
" clude either Hope or Charity from being always joined as
" infeparable mates with Faith, in the man that is juftified ;
" or Works from being added, as neceffary duties required of
" every juftified man : but to fhew that Faith is the only hand
" which putteth on CHRIST to juftification ; and CHRIST the
" only garment which being fo put on covereth the fhame of
" our defiled natures, hideth the imperfection of our Works,
" and preferveth us blamelefs in the fight of GOD."

Works till then have in them the nature of fin.
See ART. XIII. which has this title prefixed to it—
Of Works done before Juſtification. " Works done
" before the Grace of CHRIST, and the inſpiration
" of his Spirit, are not pleaſant to GOD, foraſmuch
" as they ſpring not of Faith in JESUS CHRIST;
" neither do they make men meet to receive
" Grace, or, as the ſchool-authors ſay, deſerve
" grace of congruity : yea, rather, for that they
" are not done as GOD hath willed and command-
" ed them to be done, we doubt not but they
" have the nature of fin *."

How different is the language of this truly
ſcriptural Article, as well as that of the XIth,
which declares in expreſs words that we are juſtified by Faith only, from that of a Sermon preached
before

---

* The Rev. Dr R———H, Preſident of *C. C. C.* and Lady
Margaret's Profeſſor of Divinity, objected to Mr MIDDLETON,
that he heard he denied the neceſſity of good Works; adding,
that certainly good Works were a part of our Juſtification. To
which Mr M. replied to this effect ; " that he by no means de-
" graded good Works, or denied the neceſſity of them as fruits
" and evidences of juſtifying Faith, ſpringing from love to GOD,
" but denied that they were previous to, or any part or condi-
" tion of Juſtification, which was by Faith alone."
Whoever will read the Eleventh Article, which ſays, that *we
are juſtified by Faith only*; the Twelfth, which declares, that *a
lively Faith may be evidently known by producing good Works*; and
the Thirteenth, which affirms, that *Works before Juſtification are
not pleaſant to God, but have in them the nature of fin*, will be
able to judge whether the old Doctor or the young Culprit ſpoke
moſt agreeable to the Church of England.

before the U——y a few years ago, by the V—
P—— of a certain H—l, and publiſhed at the
requeſt of Mr V—C——, with this barefaced
title, NO ACCEPTANCE WITH GOD BY FAITH
ONLY: from which Sermon I extract verbatim
what follows:

" In vain do we talk of being juſtified, without
" being previouſly ſanctified.—We ought firmly
" to believe, that no perſons can be juſtified in
" the ſight of GOD by Faith alone, as it is ſtrictly
" taken, without the other virtues which CHRIST
" hath required together with it, in order to that
" end.—The hope that maketh not aſhamed, and
" on which we may ſafely lean, is born of, and
" acknowledges good Works for its parent."

Now I appeal to every one who is at all acquainted with the controverſy between the popiſh
and reformed Churches in the point of Juſtification, whether they find any expreſſions in the
writers of the former communion more derogatory
from the great Salvation of JESUS CHRIST, than
thoſe quoted out of this Sermon.

WHO could have ſuppoſed it poſſible that another article of accuſation againſt any of theſe ſix
ſtudents ſhould be, that they held the Influences
of the HOLY SPIRIT neceſſary to conſtitute every
                                              one

one a child of God *; and that till we have this
Spirit we can do nothing? I fay, who could
have fuppofed this poffible, when our Lord himfelf fays, " Without me (and he is only prefent
by his Spirit) " ye can do nothing ;" and when
the Church of *England* ordains no Minifters but
fuch as declare " they are inwardly moved by the
" Holy Ghoft to take upon them the care of
" fouls ;

* After Mr Kay had been convicted of believing that the
efficacious Influences of the Spirit were neceffary to conftitute
every one a child of God; it was proclaimed in Court by the
Rev. Dr ——— " Is there any body here that ever heard Mr
" Middleton fay any thing about the Spirit?" After a fhort
filence, Mr H———n the Tutor, called to the Reverend Mr
B———n, to give his teftimony, and he accordingly ftood
forth; but when this Gentleman began to open his budget,
he hummed,—and hawed,—and muttered fomething about
walking up *Heddington-hill*,—faying,—'tis a long time ago—I
have forgot.—In fhort, he made fuch a muddled piece of work,
that inftead of being able to bring any charge againft Mr M—n
on this point, he feemed much in the cafe of thofe who when
they were afked by St Paul, whether they had received the
holy Ghoft fince they believed? made anfwer, " We have not
fo much as heard whether there be any holy Ghoft."

It fhould be obferved, that though Mr Middleton is charged
with having faid, that *we muft fit down and wait for the Spirit*,
that he really never made ufe of any fuch expreffion, and abfolutely denied it before the Judgment-feat; yet Dr N———l,
who officiated as Secretary, put it down to his account : therefore, true or not, *what he had written, he had written* : and
this moft falfe accufation (together with the equally falfe ones,
of his having denied the neceffity of good works, and of Mr
Grove having preached in a Barn) were fent to the Chancellor as actual facts.

" fouls † ;" and teaches us to pray for the infpiration grace and influences of the holy Spirit, no
lefs than ten, times every Sabbath morning ; not
to mention the many Collects wherein the total
depravity and weaknefs of man is acknowledged,
and we are directed to look and wait for help from
above, through the Spirit *.   Now what a folemn
                                    " mockery

† Inftead of the queftion " Do you truft that you are inwardly moved by the holy Ghoft to take upon you this office and miniftration ?" Might it not prevent the frequency of ANANIAS's
and SAPHIRA's fin if the Bifhop was to afk as follows ? " Do
" you truft that you are inwardly moved by the hope of a
" good living, to take upon you this office and miniftration ?"

* 1. Let us befeech him to grant us true repentance and
his holy Spirit.

2. Take not thy holy Spirit from us.

3. Replenifh him with the grace of thy holy Spirit.

4. Endue them with thy holy Spirit.

5. Send down upon them the healthful Spirit of thy Grace.

6. O GOD the holy Ghoft, have mercy upon us miferable
Sinners.

7. That we may bring forth the Fruits of the Spirit.

8. Endue us with the Grace of thy holy Spirit.

9. The fellowfhip of the holy Ghoft be with you all.

10. Cleanfe the thoughts of our hearts by the infpiration of
thy holy Spirit.

St AUGUSTINE, fpeaking of thofe words of our LORD, " With-
" out me ye can do nothing ;" bids us obferve, that it is not
faid without me ye can do but little, or no great matters, but
without me ye can do NOTHING.   And this is not only the language of Scripture and Fathers, but of our own Church alfo.
In the Collect for the firft Sunday after *Trinity*, fhe makes ufe
of this expreffion.—" Through the weaknefs of our mortal na-
" ture we can do No good thing without thee." In the Collect
for the ninth Sunday after *Trinity*, fhe teaches us thus to pray,
                                    " Grant

mockery of Almighty God muſt they be guilty of, who take theſe expreſſions in their lips, and yet at the ſame time believe in their hearts, that we are not now to expect to be inſpired, taught, led, influenced and comforted by the holy Ghoſt ; nay, who, after having offered up theſe petitions in the Deſk, declare from the Pulpit that it is a proof of Frenzy and Enthuſiaſm to believe God will vouchſafe an Anſwer to them.

AND now, Men, Brethren and Fathers, are theſe things ſo? and if they are, what ſhould be done unto the men who are advocates for apoſtate man's Free Will? who deny the doctrines of Election, Perſeverance, Juſtification by Faith alone, and the neceſſity of the influences of the holy Spirit? By the Word of God, if they continue to do ſo after the *ſecond* admonition, they are to be rejected as *heretics.*—By the Statutes of the Univerſity, they are liable to expulſion, as broachers of falſe doctrine, enemies to the Church, and diſturbers of the public peace.—By the King's Declaration, prefixed to the XXXIX Articles, they are ſubject to his Majeſty's diſpleaſure, and

to

" Grant to us, Lord, the Spirit to think and do always ſuch
" things as be rightful ; that we, who cannot do ANY THING
" that is good without thee," &c. So alſo in another Collect ;
" O Lord, who ſeeſt that of ourſelves we have NO power to
" help ourſelves." And again, " Grant, that we who lean
" ONLY on the hope of thy heavenly grace," &c.—Quotations
of this ſort were endleſs, as the whole book of Common-Prayer
breathes this humble Spirit.

to ecclefiaftical cenfures.—And by the Fifth Canon, they are liable to be, *ipfo facto*, excommunicated, as being Impugners of the XXXIX Articles ; and not to be reftored but by the Archbifhop, upon their repentance, and revocation of
their wicked errors.—But alas! *Quid leges fine
moribus vanæ proficiunt.*

BUT it was moreover objected againft thefe
young men, that they were connected with Mr
FLETCHER *, Mr NEWTON, Mr DAVIES, Mr
VENN, Mr TOWNSEND, &c. who were reputed
Methodifts.—And wherefore fo reputed ? Why
becaufe they believe the Articles they have fubfcribed to : and inftead of fpending their time in
idlenefs and fenfual indulgence, or in talking of
raifing their Tythes, and how much fuch and
fuch a Minifter's Living brings in, whether fuch
and fuch benefices are tenable together, where the
beft port wine, and cheapeft Curates are to be
had, and whether there is eafy duty or not, preach
feveral times in the week, go to their Parifhioners
houfes, inquire into the ftate of their fouls, are
" inftant in feafon and out of feafon, rebuke, ex-
" hort

* Mr MATTHEWS being queftioned before the Court concerning Mr FLETCHER, gave a particular account of his holy
mortified life, and zealous labors for the good of fouls. So *there
needed no further witnefs.*—Mr FLETCHER was immediately
dubbed an incorrigible Methodift; and Mr MATTHEWS himfelf juftly expelled for having been with fuch an enemy to good
works, and fo dangerous a difturber of the peace and good
order of the Church.

" hort and comfort," as occafion requires ; and, if need be, are ready to lay down their lives for the flock. If the Gentlemen who paffed the fevere fentence of Expulfion on thefe fix ftudents have any acts of immorality to alledge againft the abovementioned Clergymen, let them ftand forth and produce them : If they can prove that they hold or teach any doctrines either repugnant to the word of God, or to the avowed tenets of the Eftablifhed Church, or have any ways acted contrary to the difcipline of the latter, let them now make it appear ; otherwife what an indelible blot muft it caft upon their characters, as heads of the U——y, and fathers of the Church, to have made men, who ought to be held in the higheft honor for their works fake, fo much the objects of public contempt and reproach, as to punifh a connection with them with the moft cruel and ignominious fentence their laws could inflict ?

If indeed it could have been proved, that any of the youths under their care were connected with Clergymen of loofe morals, or with fuch as had fo little fenfe of their facred truft, as for the fake of filthy lucre, to become Pluralifts or idle Non-refidents ; if there was any reafon to fufpect that they might be acquainted with fuch as had impioufly and hypocritically fet their hands to doc- trines which in their hearts they never affented to, and were likely to poifon their young minds with the

the blasphemies of ARIUS*, PELAGIUS, SOCINUS or ARMINIUS, or were maintainers of the Popish heresies of Free-will, universal Redemption, falling from Grace, justification by Works, either in whole or in part, or who denied the necessity of the influences of the Spirit to constitute every one a child of GOD; I say, if but a suspicion should have arisen in the minds of these great and learned men, who bear rule and authority in the University, that any Under-graduates, especially such as were intended for holy Orders, were intimately acquainted with any such dangerous Heretics and Schismatics as these, (who may be justly looked upon to be as much incendiaries in the Church, as the famed Mr W— is in the State) it would have been highly becoming the wisdom of Mr F. V—

* By the 1st, 9th and 10th of Wm. III. for preventing the horrible crimes of Blasphemy and Profaneness, " Whoso- " ever shall deny any one of the persons in the Trinity to be " GOD, or shall deny in preaching or writing the doctrines of " the blessed Trinity, as set forth in the XXXIX Articles, shall " be incapable of holding any ecclesiastical office." But these Acts of Parliament have of late years lain dormant, and now a direct contrary punishment is frequently passed upon such profane Blasphemers, _viz._ a promotion to the highest ecclesiastical offices, as we may instance in the cases of the late Rev. and Learned Dr SAMUEL CLARKE, Dr SYKES, the Right Rev. Fathers in GOD Dr BENJAMIN HOADLY, late Lord Bishop of _Winchester_, and Dr CLAYTON, late Lord Bishop of _Clogher_ in _Ireland_; not to mention the renowned Archbishop TILLOTSON, who, if he did not go the lengths of the before mentioned Gentlemen, kindly wished the Church " well rid of the Athanasian Creed." &c. &c. &c. &c. &c. &c. &c. &c. &c. &c. &c. &c. &c. &c. &c. &c. &c. &c. &c. &c. &c. &c. &c.

V— C—— and his affeffors. to have paffed fome
cenfure upon them.—But,—" O tell it not in *Gath!*
publifh it not in the ftreets of *Afkelon!*"—Let
filence conceive, what grief forbids to utter †.

I have now gone through every particular charge
againft each of the young men; and whofoever
hath attended to thefe charges will readily fee that
moft,

† Although I confefs that I do not fee how any perfon can
be in a good ftate who denies the neceffity of the Spirit's influences to quicken, renew, fanctify, enlighten, and comfort
the foul; or who joins any thing with CHRIST in the matter
of juftification; yet I would not be underftood to intimate, that
believing the doctrines of perfonal Election and final Perfeverance is effential to falvation; being well affured that there
are and have been many eminent chriftians who hold univerfal redemption and falling from grace. What I mean to infift
upon, is, that the Church of *England* is certainly calviniftical,
and that the moft eminent of her divines, who lived neareft the
reformation, were of calviniftical principles. That therefore
if any cenfures were inflicted, they ought rather to have been
upon thofe who maintained the doctrines for which BARRET
was called to account by Mr. Vice-Chancellor and the heads
of houfes in Queen ELIZABETH's time, than upon fuch who,
had they been members of the Univerfity at the fame period
when BARRET was, would have met with the higheft approbation and efteem.

I the rather mention this, becaufe it hath been objected
againft me that I bore too hard upon fuch as denied Election
and Perfeverance: but perhaps thefe objections will not appear
fo well founded, if we reflect that thofe parts of the book which
moftly carry this afpect, are not my own words, but prece-
dents of the proceedings of thofe in power againft fuch as were
oppofers of thefe doctrines; or elfe quotations from the writings
of our firft Reformers.

-moſt, if not all of them, might equally have been brought againſt our Lord, the Apoſtles, and Evangeliſts.

1ſt, *They were moſt of them bred to trades.*—JESUS the Carpenter, LUKE the Phyſician and Painter, MATTHEW the Publican, PAUL the Tent-maker, PETER, ANDREW, JAMES and JOHN, the Fiſhermen.

2dly, *They were* (moſt of them) *very deficient in the knowledge of the learned languages.*—Much more ſo than any of the expelled youths.

3dly, *They all uſed extempore prayer* *; and if they did not hear one HEWET a Stay-maker (although a layman) pray extempore in a private houſe, as was objected againſt Mr KAY; yet they heard one BARTIMEUS, a poor old blind Lay-beggar, pray extempore by the way-ſide, which was certainly much worſe. And that ring-leader of the ſect, PAUL the Tent-maker, was himſelf a notorious promoter of this kind of prayer, and of the enthuſiaſtic cuſtom of Hymn-ſinging; for we find, that he even kneeled down on the ſea-ſhore, without either book, haſſock or velvet cuſhion, and prayed with his friends who

F 2   accompanied

---

* Since the publication of the firſt edition of this book, I have come to the knowledge of the following anecdote, *viz.* that the Rev. Mr HIGSON, who was ſo much diſpleaſed at the young men for uſing extempore prayer, in a religious qualm which ſeized him in a fit of illneſs a few years ago, deſired one of his ſerious pupils to pray by him EXTEMPORE, which he accordingly did.

accompanied him to the Ship. And then for
finging of hymns, he has given an undifguifed
exhortation to the ufe of it ; " Let the word of
CHRIST dwell in you richly in all wifdom ;
teaching and admonifhing one another in pfalms
and HYMNS and fpiritual fongs, finging with
grace in your hearts to the LORD," *Col.* iii. 16.
So it appears that our LORD, and every one of
the Apoftles, were Hymn-fingers ; for thus it is
written, " when they had fung an hymn they
" departed into the mount of Olives."--It makes
nothing againft us that JUDAS was a wolf in
fheeps-clothing, who in his heart hated the
Hymns, but loved the money-bag.

4*thly*, *They all attended illicit Conventicles.*—And it
was in one of thefe Conventicles that this fame
peftilent mover of fedition, this turbulent fel-
low, this fomenter of divifions in families, the
tent-maker, even out-preached all our modern
Enthufiafts ; for we find he continued his *extempore* fpeech until midnight, and preached poor
EUTYCHUS faft afleep, whofe cuftom of napping,
more than of PAUL's preaching, has fince been
followed by many great and dignified Divines,
as may be feen at the U———y-Church of Saint
M—y moft Sundays in the afternoon through-
out the year, but particularly on *Gaudy-days,* by
thofe who can find time to leave the common
room, and attend their refpective evening prayers in Chapel.

5*tbly*, If we allow the Church of *England* to be in
the right, JESUS and, all the Apoſtles and
Evangeliſts held the doctrines of Election—
Juſtification by Faith alone without Works—
Once a child of GOD, always a child of GOD—
That we can do nothing without the Spirit,
whoſe efficacious influences are neceſſary to
conſtitute every one a child of GOD—and they,
as well as Mr KAY, *have endeavoured to draw
others into theſe Opinions.*

6*tbly*, Mr VENN, Mr NEWTON, Mr TOWNSEND,
Mr FLETCHER and Mr DAVIES, having no exiſt-
ence in thoſe Days, it cannot be ſaid that our
LORD and his Apoſtles had any connection with
them, but no doubt they were connected with
many of the ſame Methodiſtical caſt, and whom
the high Prieſt and Rulers, Scribes and Pha-
riſees, Lawyers * and Doctors, looked upon to
be as great enemies to the Church, and as dreadful diſturbers of the public tranquillity, as the
abovementioned Clergymen were by Mr V—
C—— and his Aſſeſſors.

AND now to bring this matter to a concluſion:
If the doctrines of Election, Perſeverance, Juſti-

fication

---

* *ɩoμιxoì*, expounders of the law.

fication by Faith alone, Assurance of Salvation, and the necessity of the influences of the Spirit to constitute every one a child of God, are the known, avowed, received tenets of the Reformation, and of the Church of *England*; and if the doctrines of Free-will, Universal Redemption, falling from grace, Conditional Salvation, Justification partly by Faith and partly by Works, or (as the Bishop of Meaux expresses it, in his artful book intitled *l' Exposition de la doctrine de l' Eglise Catholique)* by works wrought by the Spirit through Faith, are the known, avowed, received tenets of the Church of *Rome*, and were abhorred by our Reformers, as being *doctrines of devils, and limbs of antichrist*, which caused the chaste spouse of Christ to separate from the Babylonish Whore; then, from whence are we fallen? And how justly may we be alarmed at the great increase of Popery in our land? But from what quarter our danger is to be apprehended, whether from private Mass-houses, or from public and authorized chairs of Oratory, let matter of fact and sad experience determine. Alas! the doctrine of Transubstantiation is an harmless error, compared with that which would make the Almighty Spirit of God dependent on the will of the fallen creature, or give man's righteousness a place on Christ's throne, and share with Him in the great work of justifying a sinner before God.

IF

IF then the Church of *England* be deemed a true apoftolical Church, let us be zealous in her defence. If fhe be deemed a falfe Church, let thofe who think her fo, at once burn her Articles, Homilies, and Common Prayer at *Charing-Crofs*. This would be acting openly and without hypocrify: then might the true friends of her communion be diftinguifhed from thofe fubtle ferpents who lurk within her-bofom only to prey upon her vitals; and whilft they are throwing duft into the eyes of the deluded multitude, by crying out " *The Church,* " *The Church,* the temple of the LORD are we ;" would overturn her very foundation, if the promife of GOD had not engaged that " the gates of " hell fhall never prevail againft her."—But, for the fake of filthy lucre, to carry on a folemn farce of fubfcribing to Articles, which many of the fubfcribers no more believe, than they do Mother Goofe's Tales; and then to form excufes for this horrid mockery, by calling them Articles of *Peace,* inftead of Articles of *Faith,* is fuch a degree of impious jefuitical equivocation, as without fpeedy repentance muft draw down the juft vengeance of a long-fuffering GOD upon our land.

I know it will be thought by many that I have declared my fentiments too plainly ; but let any one read the very fharp expreffions of Him, who neverthelefs was meek and lowly in heart, againft the high Priefts and Rulers of the fynagogue, the Scribes and Pharifees, Lawyers and Doctors, who whilft they were the bittereft enemies of true god-

liness, set themselves up for the orthodox instruc-
tors of the age.—Let any one read the nervous ex-
clamations of that courageous Champion of the
Reformation, MARTIN LUTHER, against the popish advocates for Justification by Works, and
the denyers of the free imputation of CHRIST's
Righteousness to sinners, and then let them tell me
that I have spoken things which ought to have been
concealed.

The following is the copy of a Letter written
about two Years ago by Mr MIDDLETON to
the Right Hon. and Right Rev. Father in
GOD Lord JAMES BEAUCLERK Bishop of *Hereford*; which Letter, as it was read by Mr M.
at the trial, I have annexed, as a proof of that
Gentleman's intentions, had he not been expelled and refused Ordination.

My LORD,

THOUGH I have not been so happy as to
succeed in my application to your Lordship for
ordination, yet I hope you will have no objection
to return me the papers I left with your Lordship,
as I flatter myself that my future conduct and regularity may intitle me to that favor from your Lordship or some other of the Bishops, which I acknowledge my own imprudencies have at present justly
deprived

deprived me of *.—However, I humbly hope your Lordſhip will permit me to plead my youth and inexperience as ſome mitigation of my errors, and to aſſure you, that I have for ſome time been convinced of the propriety and neceſſity of obſerving the ſtricteſt order and regularity; and that if I had now met with your Lordſhip's approbation, that I ſhould have made it my conſtant endeavour not to have rendered myſelf unworthy of it, but in all things to have paid the utmoſt regard to the doctrine and diſcipline of that excellent Church in which I am ſo deſirous of the honor of being a Miniſter.

I have the higheſt ſenſe of the great condeſcenſion and kindneſs of good Lord VERE for intereſting himſelf in my behalf; but as your Lordſhip has not thought proper to comply with his requeſt, I am willing to take your refuſal as the juſt reward of my paſt folly and imprudence, however contrary my intention was to have acted for the future. I am,

My LORD,

Your Lordſhip's moſt obedient,

and moſt humble Servant,

ERASMUS MIDDLETON.

* Alluding particularly to his having preached in a Chapel unordained.

POSTSCRIPT.

A Pamphlet, intitled, *A vindication of the proceedings against the six members of* Edmund Hall, has lately appeared, which confirms the affertions I have made, beyond any thing that could have been written in defence of the young men; infomuch that if I did not believe the Reverend Mr WHITEFIELD had more Religion and Honefty than to be guilty of fuch a knavifh action, I fhould be inclined to think (and am not fingular in the opinion) that the author was fome perfon employed by him to expofe Mr V— C—— and his Affeffors, by writing a weak, or an ironical defence of their conduct. However, be that as it will, perhaps this poor catch-penny Gentleman was in want of a dinner; and certainly all the young men are much obliged to him for the fervice he has done their caufe, and particularly myfelf, for having furnifhed me with a motto to *Pietas Oxonienfis.*

But let us enter a little into the merits of his performance.—Our Author, who feems of the Pelagian or Arminian leaven, begins with obferving, that " to profefs openly our religious principles, " and to worfhip GOD in fuch manner as feems to

" us

" us moſt acceptable to him, are juſtly eſteemed
" a noble branch of the liberties of this country ;
" that we claim it as our birth-right, as one
" of thoſe glorious privileges bought by the
" ſwords, and ſealed with the blood of our noble
" anceſtors."

What he means by all this pompous nonſenſical
flouriſh, I am at a loſs to find out.—That many
glorious Goſpel-truths were ſealed with the blood
of our noble anceſtors, is certain, but then theſe
truths are the very ſame which this writer ranks
in the liſt of methodiſtical hereſies.—As to any *religious principles* or *privileges* being bought by
the ſword in this nation, I profeſs myſelf ſo utterly
ignorant of the hiſtory of my own country as not
to know that this was ever the caſe, even from the
firſt dawn of the Reformation by WICKLIFF under
EDWARD the third, to its perfect eſtabliſhment in
the reign of Queen ELIZABETH.—The grand im-
poſtor MAHOMET did indeed propagate his religion
by the power of the temporal ſword, but the ſub-
jects of the Prince of peace have other weapons to
fight with, namely, *the ſword of the Spirit, the
breaſt-plate of Righteouſneſs, the ſhield of Faith, and
the helmet of Salvation* ; but theſe, I fear, are over-
grown with ruſt ; and who has not heard that the
uſe of them is in a manner prohibited by *the new
regulations* at a certain famous U——y ?

One thing which ſeems to give particular offence to this writer is, that ſome of the expelled
members were of low extraction or circumſtances,
and

and that they fhould *prefume to rank with perfons of the moft refpectable families in the kingdom* * ; yet in

* I fhould be glad to know whether our author means to rank Mr H——N the Tutor among thefe *Gentlemen of refpectable family*, from whom any accufations againft the young men for having been of mean birth or circumftances come with a very ill grace, as would clearly appear, if I was to lay before the public his private hiftory and various metamorphofes, of which I know much more than he is aware;—*O quantum mutatus ab illo!* I fhould alfo be glad to be informed, whether he means to include a certain drunken Infidel, who was admitted an evidence againft certain fober religious young men, at a certain tribunal, erected in a certain U——y ; which drunken Infidel, for ought he himfelf can tell, may indeed be of a more *refpectable family* than any Gentleman in *Oxford*, as he knows not his parents to this moment, having been a poor foundling beggar-boy, and from that condition received into the houfe of an honeft Hatter to run on errands; from whence he became the fcout of an Apothecary in *Leicefter-fields*, to trot about with pills and purging potions ; after which he was taken into the houfe of a worthy pious Clergyman, who is a Schoolmafter, where he taught children Reading and Arithmetic. Here he vigoroufly maintained his Deiftical principles, till the Maid-fervant having the misfortune to be with child, people were fo cenforious as to believe him to be the Father, which occafioned the difmiffion both of him and her. However, he af-terwards made her an honeft woman, (as we fay,) and fhe getting a good place in a Jews family, was enabled to contribute towards his fupport. But as he has actually been OR-DAINED TO A CURE OF SOULS fince this went to prefs, [pray mark well, p. 31.] and declares he will not reft till he is a Doctor in Divinity ; it is to be hoped that he will not be chargeable to the poor woman much longer.

A Gentleman who has known this Hero feveral years, told me that one ftratagem whereby he endeavoured to creep into the favor of thofe whom he thought could be ferviceable to

his

in the very next fentence he is not lefs enraged, becaufe two of them were Gentlemen of independent fortunes, and could afford to put on Gentlemen Commoners gowns.—[See here, the very fpirit of the old Pharifees : " JOHN the Baptift came neither eating nor drinking, and he hath a devil : CHRIST came both eating and drinking, and behold, a gluttonous man and a wine-bibber, a friend of publicans and finners."] However, he is a little miftaken in the fact, for only one of the expelled members was a Gentleman-Commoner, though two of that gown were accufed.

Our writer undertakes to give an explanation of the Statutes of the Univerfity, and of the Articles of the Church, in which he fhews the moft profound ignorance both of the one and of the other.

his temporal interefts, was, by firft difputing with them in defence of his Infidel opinions, and then making them believe that by their arguments he was convinced of his own errors.— This puts me in mind of what is called by our Englifh Sailors at *Naples*, WHITEWASHING. Now this *Whitewafhing* confifts in making a temporary profeffion of the Popifh religion, and fubmitting to all the forms enjoined ; for which, if the party *Whitewafhed* were before an Heretic or Proteftant, he received a reward of about two fequins ; and I am credibly informed that fome of our Britifh Tars have frequently undergone this ceremony of *Whitewafhing*.—Another anecdote told me by a perfon of undoubted veracity concerning this Gentleman, is, that being afked why he went into orders as he did not believe the Bible ? He replied, that he might as well be paid for reading that book as any other.

other †. The twenty-third Article, which declares the unlawfulneſs of unordained perſons adminiſtering the ſacraments and preaching in the ſtated *public* congregation, he interprets as laying a prohibition upon all members of the eſtabliſhed Church from reading a Sermon or giving an Exhortation in a private houſe to a few ſerious people, as ſome of the young men occaſionally did, ranking it all under the notion of public illicit preaching.—He alſo inſiſts upon it, that theſe ſtudents were liable to expulſion by that ſtatute of the Univerſity, *De conventiculis illicitis reprimendis,* for holding and propagating doctrines contrary to the thirty-nine Articles of the Church of *England*; among which erroneous doctrines he ranks Juſtification by Faith alone without works; the neceſſity of the influences of the Spirit; and once a child of God, always a child of God.—Now then it is certainly granted by this author, that whereſoever or by whomſoever any doctrines contrary to the Church of *England* are maintained and preached, all ſuch places are illicit conventicles, and the Preachers at them, and the Frequenters of them, liable to expulſion, as much as BARRET was; but as we have moſt clearly and fully proved that the above mentioned doctrines are the pure, avowed, fundamental doctrines of that Church,

consequently

† If our vindicator knows nothing elſe, he knows how to ſcoff at religion, and has learned the ſhoe-black language of ſneering at the *pious youths* and *worthy babes in grace,* as aptly as if he had been brought up to it from his cradle.

confequently whofoever holds or preaches any
others, or is prefent where any others are held
and preached, ought (according to this writer's
own interpretation of the Statutes) to be driven
from the boundàries of the Univerfity by the Vicechancellor, as an Heretic, Schifmatic, &c *. —
Should then that unhappy time arrive when Mr
V— C———, and his Affeffors, after the example of
this fame poor BARRET, not only fhould ceafe
to preach thefe doctrines, but fhew themfelves to
be open notorous impugners of them ; then, I fay,
according to our ingenious pamphleteer's own
conclufions, thefe great and learned men would
ftand expofed to all the charges of Herefy and
Schifm ; and may we not tremble for the confe-
quences? might not our Colleges be in danger of
an

* " Si quis aliquod dogma CONTRA DOCTRINAM (vel difci-
" plinam) Ecclefiæ Anglicanæ defenderit, &c. —— ab aula
" expellatur."
" If any one fhall defend any tenet contrary to the doctrine
" (as well as difcipline) of the Church of *England*, let him be
" expelled from the Hall."
In like manner the Statute which declares the office of the
Vicechancellor, enacts,—" UtHereticos, Schifmaticos, et quof-
" cunque alios minus recte de fide Catholica, et DOCTRINA vel
" difciplina Ecclefiæ Anglicanæ fentientes, procul a fihibus
" Univerfitatis amandandos curet."
Of this take the author's own tranflation. " That he (*viz.*
the V— C———) " fhall take care to banifh from the boundaries
" of the Univerfity all Heretics, Schifmatics, and all others hold-
" ing doctrines inconfiftent with the Catholic Faith, and the
" DOCTRINE or difcipline of the Church of *England*."

an utter defertion, and an almoft general Expulfion enfue?

Our author concludes his performance with one
of the higheft encomiums upon Mr. WHITEFIELD
which one man can poffibly pay another. He
affirms that the only reafon why that Gentleman
defends the young men, is becaufe he himfelf did
the fame things when, young; that is, he was
addicted to prayer, reading the fcriptures, finging
of hymns, exhorting his neighbours, adhering to
the Articles of the Church, was connected with
laborious parifh Minifters, &c. Now this eloge
is fo much beyond any thing which Mr WHITE-
FIELD would have faid of himfelf, that the writer
has put it out of all difpute which fide he means
to fupport. But if after all, any fhould ftill be
of opinion, that he really intends to blame Mr
WHITEFIELD for thefe things, then every fcrap
of dirt he cafts upon that Gentleman for praying,
reading, expounding, finging hymns, believing
the doctrines of the church of *England*, &c. is a
tacit implication that our wife vindicator is totally
free from all fuch old fafhioned cuftoms.

One word more and I have done.—If any Anfwer is made to this Pamphlet, let it be obferved
that there are three very material points, on which
I principally ground the caufe I have defended,
and therefore I thus publickly call upon the writer
of fuch Anfwer not to pafs them over.

1ft,

1st, Let him make it appear that I have mif-
reprefented any one fact relative to the Trial
and Expulfion of the young men; as I am
not afraid moft folemnly to call G o d to
witnefs to the truth of what I have afferted,
according to the beft information I have
been able to procure; and do moreover declare, that I have rather extenuated than
aggravated, as well by omitting to mention
the haughty overbearing treatment thefe youths
met with at their Trial *, and the prying im-
pertinent queftions then afked them about
their private concerns, notwithftanding the
meek fubmiffive behaviour they fhewed, as by
drawing a veil over the moral characters of
certain perfons, who have been very active
againft them, when it was in my power to
have expofed them moft feverely ;—but

Non tali auxilio nec defenforibus iftis
Tempus eget.

2d, Let the writer of the Reply prove (if he
can) that the doctrines which thefe young
men were expelled for holding, are not the
pure received doctrines of the Reformation,
and of the Church of *England.*—Let him

G   alfo

---

* When the Bifhops, Cranmer, Ridley, and Latimer
had their mock trials and examinations at *Oxford,* they were
infulted, hiffed at, laughed at, and pufhed from fide to fide
by their adverfaries, and no attention was paid to what they
faid on their own behalf. How far the cafe of the young men
was fimilar to theirs, I refer to the confciences of thofe prefent.

alſo tell me what he thinks of Barret's
caſe; and whether all perſecution is confined
to primitive times.

3d, Let him ſhew why Mr Venn, Mr Newton,
Mr Townsend, Mr Davies, and Mr
Fletcher, were called Methodiſts *; and let
ſome particular reaſons be alledged, why a
connection with theſe Gentlemen ſhould be
puniſhed with the cruel ſhameful ſentence
of Expulſion; for if to be acquainted with
them be ſo heinous a crime, certainly they
themſelves deſerve nothing leſs than the halter
and the gibbet.

A ſolution to the following Queries is alſo
requeſted.

1. Why was the teſtimony of the pious and
learned Dr Dixon in behalf of the young
men ſet at nought, and that of an avowed
Infidel againſt them received?
2. Why was an avowed Infidel diſmiſſed with a
reprimand only, upon the plea of drunkenneſs, and ſince admitted into holy Orders,
when, it is a received maxim in our Laws,
that *Drunkenneſs excuſeth no crime*; then certainly

* Though only the two laſt of theſe laborious exemplary
Miniſters were mentioned in the Articles read at the Expulſion
in the Chapel, yet their names were all brought up at the
Trial, as propagators, aiders, and abettors of Methodiſm and
Enthuſiaſm.

tainly not that of Blasphemy, which is punish-
able by Pillory, Fine and Imprisonment?———
See the Cases quoted in BURN's *Ecclef. Law,*
particularly that of WOOLSTON, who wrote
and spoke AGAINST THE MIRACLES OF OUR
LORD, but I do not find that he declared
every man must be a knave or a fool who
believed them, nor *that he added Drunkenness
or Fornication to Blasphemy.*

3. Since it is also an established rule in the Laws
of *England; Nemo seipsum tenetur accusare,*
" No man is obliged to accuse himself;"
Why were the young men questioned in
their own particular cases, and what was thus
extorted from their own mouths put down
against them?

A WORD

A WORD TO THE

MONTHLY REVIEWERS.

GENTLEMEN,

THAT you may not complain of my doing
you any injuftice by a mifreprefentation of
what you are pleafed to fay of PIETAS OXONIENSIS,
I fhall tranfcribe your own words, and then make
a few reflections which are evidently deducible
from them.

" This (*viz.* PIETAS OXONIENSIS) is a well
" digefted and fpecious defence of the Students.
" We look upon it to be a pamphlet of fuch
" dangerous tendency that it ought to be fully
" anfwered and refuted by the Gentlemen of
" *Oxford*, who are fo freely attacked in it. We
" have not lately met with fo able a vindication
" of orthodoxy and modern fanaticifm ; and we
" cannot but apprehend, that if its contents are
" not properly expofed and refuted, fuch a per-
" formance may impofe on and miflead many an
" unwary reader. The progrefs of Methodifm
" among us is now become fo confiderable, that
" it feems to be high time for rational religion
" and common fenfe to keep a good watch and
" defend themfelves againft its encroachments,
" left we be again overwhelmed by an inundation
" of pious barbarifm worfe than that of thofe
" fpiritual Goths and Vandals the Monks."
Monthly Review for June, 1768.

In the firft place, Gentlemen, permit me to
obferve that the great compliment you are fo
kind

kind as to pay me on the ability of my performance was as much unexpected as your declarations
of its *dangerous tendency* were apprehended. To
tell you the truth, I always fufpected you had a
fly affection for Infidelity, and confequently no
fmall hatred for orthodoxy ; but now you have
fpoken out, and put the matter beyond fufpicion,
for by ranking orthodoxy with fanaticifm, you
have given us a plain intimation what you mean
by *rational religion* and *common fenfe, viz.* heterodoxy and infidelity, for certainly thefe two muft
ever ftand in oppofition to orthodoxy, and there is
no defpifing this without being an advocate for
thofe.—And yet Meffrs the Reviewers tell us, that
" if this vindication of orthodoxy is not properly
anfwered and refuted by the Gentlemen of *Oxford*,
who are fo freely attacked in it, it is of fuch a
dangerous tendency as to be likely to miflead many
an unwary reader." Well then, our Reviewers it
feems take it for granted that thefe Reverend
Gentlemen are no more friends to orthodoxy than
themfelves, elfe they would never look to *Oxford*
for a refutation of it, nor fuppofe that thofe poor
unwary readers who may be mifled into orthodoxy
by the perufal of Pietas Oxoniensis, may be
brought back into heterodoxy, by the expected
anfwer from Mr V— C—— or any of his affeffors.
What may have caufed Meffrs the Reviewers to
entertain fuch ideas of the faith of thefe great and
learned men (who neverthelefs are each of them
diftinguifhed by the two capitals, D. D.) I take not
upon me to determine, but it is probable that the
mild reprimand beftowed on the Gentleman who
declared that " whofoever believed the miracles of
our Saviour and of Moses muft be a knave or a
fool," and the fevere treatment the orthodox youths
met

((192))

met with, may not a little have contributed towards their imbibing these notions of the principles of our U———y Doctors.

But, Gentlemen, why do you call the doctrine defended in PIETAS OXONIENSIS, *modern fanaticism?* if it is fanaticism at all, I am sure it is ancient fanaticism and reformation fanaticism, yea authorised and established fanaticism too, seeing the whole of this fanaticism is extracted from the Articles, Homilies, Liturgy and other offices of the Church of *England*, so that I have at least the comfort of being a fanatic with some of the best and greatest men that ever lived, *viz.* our first Reformers; whilst Messrs the Reviewers, by calling the quotations I have made from their compositions *pious barbarism, worse than that of those spiritual Goths and Vandals the Monks,* have evidently brought the matter to this issue, that Popery and Monkish superstition is greatly to be preferred to Protestantism, and that the *orthodoxy, methodism,* and *fanaticism,* which *rational religion and common sense ought to keep a good watch against,* are in truth and reality the pure scriptural doctrines of the Reformation, and of the Church of *England.*

And now, Gentlemen, I cannot help surmising that you have drawn yourselves and your friends the U———y Doctors, into a difficulty which you will not easily get out of; but if you will take my advice, the best method you can pursue is either to pass my remarks over in perfect silence, or else to say that you do not think them worth notice,

I am, Gentlemen,

Your very humble Servant.

F I N I S.